Pilgrims of the Mist

SHEILA STEWART MBE

is the last in the line of the Stewarts of Blair. She spent her childhood travelling all over Scotland and working on farms with her family. From 1954 she sang in concerts with her parents and her sister Cathie. She recently wrote a biography of her mother, Belle Stewart, *Queen Amang the Heather*. An acclaimed storyteller and ballad singer, she also lectures on the oral culture of the travelling people.

PILGRIMS OF THE MIST

The Stories of Scotland's Travelling People

Sheila Stewart MBE

BIRLINN

First published in 2008 by
Birlinn Limited
West Newington House
10 Newington Road
Edinburgh
EH9 1QS

www.birlinn.co.uk

Reprinted 2010

ISBN-13: 978 1 84158 752 3
ISBN-10: 1 84158 752 4

British Library Cataloguing-in-Publication Data
A catalogue record for this book is available from the British
Library

Set in Bembo at Birlinn

Printed and bound in Great Britain by
Cox & Wyman, Reading

Contents

Preface

I have written the biography of my mother, Belle Stewart, and a book on the culture of the travelling people of my own family, but still I feel that I owe something to the many other travellers from Scotland.

There are some great stories about them, which my granny, granda, my mother and father told me. I think these travellers should have a platform as well. There were many great characters among them.

Long ago, travelling people were very humble folk. They didn't have much, but they were content with what they had. They lived from day to day. If they got a bite to eat, and a tent to sleep in, they were happy. It was a free life they led. They worked on the land for the farmers, and tried to save some money to see them through the winter.

One thing the travellers liked was their dram. That is why they let every day look after itself. Some saved money, but others had a good time drinking it. They bought the drink in the shop, took it home to the camp and got pissed round the fire. They got up next morning, gave themselves a shake, and went back to work again. I just can't leave their stories out.

The travellers I have researched these stories from don't want to be recognised, and I can see their point. They think in the same way I do, and they trust me to write down their stories. They have given me permission to publish them, but they don't want to be involved with anyone else. I am so grateful to them, but people must understand that travellers are a closed community, and always will be.

These traveller storytellers come from all over Scotland. I thank every one of them for telling these stories to me.

May God bless them and keep them safe.

Sheila Stewart

Family Stories

❦

The Hanging

This is a story from my family that has never been told before. I am getting up in years, and I don't want to die before it is passed on. It was the biggest tragedy that ever happened to my family.

My granny's father was Campbell – Wee Andy Campbell they called him. This story is about his grandfather, and that is a long time ago. His name was also Andy Campbell.

Andy and his wife (I think her name was Kate), and three sons and two daughters were camping up at Loch Earn side. They had been there for a few weeks. In those days travellers weren't always moved on.

It was a hot summer's day, and Andy was tinkering away at his pots, and making scourers for cleaning pots and pans. His wife was away selling some stuff he had made in the last couple of days. The kids were playing their favourite game, exploring.

Andy stopped for a wee while to make tea and give the kids bread and butter, and for himself to have a smoke of his pipe. A clay cutty, it was. He hadn't much tobacco left, but hopefully he had enough till his wife came home from the town.

Just then, a man on horseback approached the camp. "Well, my man, I see you are smoking your pipe. Can I have some tobacco from you? I have run out."

"I would kindly give it to you, sir, but I have just put the last I have in my pipe," said Andy.

"You are a liar," said the man. "All you damn tinkers are the same. Come here to me, man. I want to talk to you, and I don't want to get off my horse."

1

So Andy approached the man on horseback, and was struck on the face with his whip. It was such a blow it made the man fall off his horse. "How dare you unsaddle me from my horse! You will pay for this, tinker."

He got a rope from the horse's saddle and tied it round Andy's waist, making sure his arms were pinned tightly. "Come with me, to be punished for your insolence."

The girls were crying and the boys were mad with anger, but they stayed quiet. Andy was dragged along the dirt road, getting many scratches on the way.

The oldest boy said, "I will go and find mammy, and tell her the news." He found her in the grocer's shop, buying messages. He told her what had happened, and she flew back to the camp.

Andy had not returned. The kids were crying their wee eyes out. "Two of you boys go and get your uncle Willie and uncle John, and tell them I want them to come straight away."

The boys ran as fast as their legs could carry them. It was her own brothers she was sending for, and the boys had two miles to go to their camp.

When they arrived, tired and breathless, they crumpled in a heap on the ground, and waited to get their breath back before they could speak. They told their uncles what had happened, and the two men made off for the camp, telling the boys to stay with their granny till they came back.

When they arrived at their sister's camp, they found her and her children lying huddled together, frightened out of their wits in case the man came back.

"You stay here wi' the wains and we will go and see what is happening."

Two hours later, they came back, saying Andy was in a terrible state. He had been beaten up, and he was lying in jail.

"You can't go and see him till the morning. That's what they said. Come back with us tonight and we will go in the morning and take you with us." So they packed up the food and a few clothes for the kids, and away they went.

Next morning, the three of them arrived at the jail about nine o'clock. They had to wait two hours till it opened. They went inside, and asked for Andy.

"Oh, you can't see him, he is being tried today."

"What for?" they asked.

"Because he is a tinker."

"But you can't hang a man for that," said Kate.

"Oh yes we can, and we will – the law says we can. We need to get rid of tinker scum."

"Well," said Kate, "I am a tinker as well." Her two brothers spoke up and said they were tinkers also.

Just at that moment a man came in, and Kate knew at once it was the man who had taken Andy away. He was arrogant and impudent.

"What have you done with my man, you cheeky bastard?" she cried.

"You swore at me, arrest her as well."

The two brothers made a breenge[1] at the man, and in a moment they were arrested too and thrown in jail beside Andy. He was so badly beaten they hardly recognised him, but he was able to speak to them.

Next morning the four of them were hanged, just for being tinkers.

There are many stories like this. The hanging of tinkers didn't end till 1964, when hanging was abolished. It is sad to think of the travellers that suffered this fate, but many tinkers died on the gallows.

1. charge

3

Mary Reid

Many, many years ago, there was a wee girl called Mary Reid. My great granny was a Reid, and this story was handed down to me from my mother's side of the family.

Mary and her parents were camped up at Prosen in Perthshire. The mother and father kept Mary inside their tent all the time, but one year some of their relations came to stay beside them for a few weeks.

Now, these relations had never seen Mary, although she was ten years of age. She was kept hidden, and the reason was that she had a club foot. As far as other travellers were concerned, that was the devil's work.

Mary's parents couldn't keep her hidden from her relations for too long, as they were staying beside them. The first night they arrived, Mary's father and mother gathered them round the fire to tell them about Mary.

"Well," said the father, "we have a wee girl, and she is ten years old, and the reason we never told youse about her was because she's no richt."

"What do you mean, she's no richt?" asked one of the women.

"Well," said the father "I think she has a club fit."

They all gasped and said, "Let us see her," expecting to see a wee monster coming out of the tent.

The father went in and brought Mary out, and she was very pretty. She had long, curly hair, which was a sandy blond. He laid her down on the grass beside every one, so that they could see her.

She was terrified sitting there with everyone staring at her.

"Let's see the fit," said one of the women. Mary's mother took off the wee cloth they had tied round it, to let them see.

4

Mary had no toes, only a big toe, and her heel was three times the height of a normal heel. Her big toe was curled flat to her instep, and wouldn't straighten.

Some of the bairns jumped back in fear, and I may say some of the adults did as well, although they tried to cover it up.

"Can she speak, or is she daft as well?"

"She can speak a wee bit, but we have just no learned her," said the mother. "We have no time for her at all. She is a decrypted[1] crater, and we just cannae take to her at all."

"We use her, really," said the father. "When we take her intae the toon wi us, folk take pity on us, and they always gi'e us money. That's the only thing she's good for."

Mary was sitting listening to what they were saying about her, and she started to scream, and to point to her mother and father. She was mumbling something, but no one could make out what she was saying.

"She's no cull[2] at a'," one of the wee lassies said. "She kens youse are all speaking about her, and she's no pleased."

"Awa, silly lassie, she kens nothing. She does that all the time."

"Maybe because youse speak aboot her all the time, it makes her angry."

"Now I am beginning to think *you're* moich,[3]" said Mary's mother.

"Dinnae you call my bairn moich," said a big fat greasy woman, with her belly hanging down between her legs. and pappies bigger than a coo's elder.[4] Her hair hadn't been combed for months, and the slavers were blinding her.

"Now calm doon," said Mary's father. "There's nae use arguing aboot it, she is simple and we a' ken that." Mary again started to scream.

The wee lassie, whose name was Nancy, knew Mary wasn't daft.

The next day the women and the men went out to do some hawking round the doors. After they had been away for a while,

1. deformed   2. stupid   3. daft   4. udder

Nancy went over to the tent where Mary was. She shouted, "Can I come in, Mary? It's me, Nancy."

She heard a type of grunt, and lifted the flap of the tent door and looked in. There was Mary sitting in the bed smiling at her. She went in and sat down, smiling back.

"I hope you don't mind me coming to see you?" Mary vigorously shook her head, and smiled again. "Never heed my mother," said Nancy, "she is aggravating at times. You do understand what I am saying, Mary?"

Mary nodded, but didn't speak, so Nancy sat there with Mary till she thought it was about time the mothers and fathers would be back. Nancy chatted on and on, and drew a smile to Mary's face more than once. "Well, I must go now Mary. I will come back tomorrow, and I am going to try and teach you to speak as well. We will be here for a few weeks yet, that's time enough, and then you can tell them all what you think of them. Alright, Mary?" Mary waved goodbye, with a smile on her face.

Every day for about a week, Nancy went to see Mary. They became very close friends, and soon Mary could say some words – "bye bye", "hello", "tea", "fire" and so on. Within a week she had come on in leaps and bounds, but the two girls never let on to anyone in the family. She was happier than she had ever been in her life, and so was Nancy.

Mary's father carried her out each night to sit around the fire, but though no one took any notice of her, she enjoyed the crack.

After another week had gone by, with Nancy's help, she could join up words to make a sentence. She still had the voice of a baby, very high and squeaky.

At the end of the second week, it was time for them to move on and go their separate ways. On the last night of their stay they bought whisky to have a wee party and a ceilidh round the fire. They were singing and telling stories and blethering.

Nancy's mother had a full skelp of whisky into her, and she was even dancing round the fire. The kids were clapping their hands, and Nancy's father cantarached[1] to her dancing. Mary burst out laughing, and immediately everything stopped. They stared at Mary, shocked that she could join in and laugh with them. "I can speak too, father," she said, in a mumbled squeaky voice.

I think everyone who was there who was drunk sobered up instantly with shock. Her mother and father suddenly saw her in a different light, and hugged her, to her delight. She had never been hugged before.

Nancy's family decided to stay on for another couple of weeks at that campsite so that Nancy could still work with Mary and get her talking. After the two weeks were up, they decided to leave the following day.

Sitting round the fire the night before they set off, they were singing and telling stories. By this time Mary's voice had got stronger, and she started to sing an old Scottish ballad. Her relatives around the fire couldn't contain themselves from crying. The song was so beautiful, and the way Mary sang, it was as if it was made for her to sing.

A month later, her father bought an old pram, and he and Mary's mother took Mary everywhere hawking with them. Mary sang, busking in the streets. She wasn't ashamed at doing this, but proud of her new achievement. She couldn't believe she had become an entertainer, and was able to make money for the family.

Mary grew up, got married and had six children, to whom she passed her songs and ballads down. Probably, I am singing them today.

1. made mouth music

The Whelks

My granny told me this story many, many years ago.

They were camped away up north near Oban, and there were a lot of travellers staying there. My grandfather was busking, but the rest of the travellers were there doing the whelks. It was a popular job for travellers, and they made a lot of money at it. Not as much as they make now from collecting them, but it wasn't too bad.

It is a cold and very wet job. They would collect the whelks from the sea shore, when the tide went out, and in these days they didn't have small boats to take them out further. They gathered what they could by wading through the water. They gathered them in baskets, then put them in sacks sometimes if they had any, but mostly in creels, and sold them to a firm in Oban. The firm would collect them. Many travellers got very sick with being in the water too much, and it made them old before their time, but it was a job and they did it.

My story starts one year when there were a lot more travellers than usual doing the whelks. The company was great, my granny said. Some of the travellers had what we call a side-kick, a man who joined the family. He would do most of the chores, going for water, cleaning the camp, and odd jobs that needed to be done, and also gather the whelks, and the money went to the family. He got fed and a wee bow tent was built for him, and they looked after him. Some travellers called them dossers.

Well, this particular family had a side-kick, and he wasn't all there. They called him Heky, though his real name was Sandy. He was a soft creature, but cheery. He wouldn't do anything unless you told him to. He was willing, but couldn't think for himself, and they had to keep reminding him what to do.

The Whelks

One day they were all out gathering whelks, and he fell into the water. It was a freezing cold day, and it was raining. They got home that night and he took ill with a severe cold. So he crawled into his tent, and he was shivering. My granny went over and gave him an extra blanket and a cup of soup. He seemed to perk up a bit, but not much. He finally fell asleep. Next morning he wasn't fit to go to the whelks, so he lay in his tent all day, with a dog for company and to keep him warm.

That night he was no better, he had a wheezy chest. My granny went over to him and put a brown ham-shank skin on his chest. That is what my family swore by for a cold. He kept it on all night, and he was fine in the morning. My granda asked him what he had done with the ham-shank skin, as he wanted to give it to his dog. "Oh, I ate it, and it tasted great," he said, "it cured me both inside and outside." Everyone in the camp just killed themselves laughing at him.

He was an awful man for climbing trees. When he wasn't working you would always find him up a tree. One day they didn't go to the whelks, because the lorry was coming to pick up the ones they had collected. It was a Saturday, and Heky announced he was going into town to have a look around, so he headed for Oban.

"Will he be alright, going into Oban by himself?" my granda asked.

"Oh yes, he will be fine," said the man he worked for.

He was away all day and all night. When he came back he said he had been in the jail.

"What were you in jail for?" asked the man he worked for.

"They said I chored.[1]"

"What did you chore?"

"Well, I went into this pub, and this man said hello to me, then he went out side for a sloosh,[2] and I thought he had gone hame, so I drank his beer. The landlord sent for the police, and they arrested me, and I was in jail all night, but the man came to the jail windy, and shouted he was going to get me when I

1. stole   2. pee

9

came oot of jail. They let me oot early this morning, and I flew back to the camp as fast as I could. Oh, what will I dae now, he will be up here looking for me?"

So he made off to the biggest tree near the camp, and speeled up it like a squirrel. "Aye," the travellers were shouting to him, "you had better hide, he will be here soon, Heky." They were laughing their heads off.

Well, the man came with two other big bully boys. They had a chat with the rest of the travellers, who told them that Heky was a bit simple, and was sorry about what he'd done. One of the travellers said to the men, "I will pay you for the pint, but I want you pretend you are going to beat him up, just to teach him a lesson."

"Where is he?" said the man who had had his drink taken.

"Do you see that big tree over there? He is at the top of that, and won't come down."

The man went and shouted up the tree, "You had better come down, or I will come up there. I climb trees for a living, and it's no problem for me to get you down."

Heky thought for a while and said, "I am no comin doon. I will drown you first!" So he took out his willie and slooshed all over the man below. Now he was getting angry again.

"Come doon, or I will come up and drag you down."

The rest of the travellers gave the man money for the beer and apologised for Heky's behaviour. Finally he headed away, but the travellers told Heky he was still there.

"What am I going to do now? I need a geer.[1]"

"You will have to come down, then," shouted the travellers.

"No me," said Heky. "I will geer my trousers first, before I come doon," and he did just that.

They shouted up to him: "The man is away now, Heky, we paid him for the beer and off he went."

"You are just sayin that to get me down," said Heky.

1. shit

So he stayed up the tree for three days, and wouldn't come down. It was hunger that made him come down off the tree in the end, that and the smell from his trousers.

The travellers were moving the next day, as the whelks were finished. Heky wanted to stay with my granny and granda, because they were going back to Ireland that year. So they said he could go with them. It took him all that day sitting in the burn to wash the mess off his arse. He was shivering but happy, he was going to Ireland.

He came out of the river, and my granny gave him a towel to dry himself. "No, no," he said, "I will roll myself in the grass till I am dry," and he did. My granda gave him a pair of plus-fours to wear, because my granda wore nothing else but plus-fours.

The Poacher

There was once a traveller man named Jimmy. He had a wife named Lizzy, and one son called after himself. He was a full-time poacher – that was his job, and that is how he made his living. He caught game and fish for the hotels and rabbits for the butcher. This couple weren't the full shilling, but very quiet and shy. My father knew them very well. They called my father Biddly, which all the travellers did then.

They lived in a place near Redgorton. It was very wooded and bushy there, which suited them just fine. It was peaceful and quiet.

All was fine and dandy with them for about six months. Then another family moved into the wood not far from them. They didn't like that one bit, but at least the other traveller wasn't a poacher, so Jimmy's job was safe.

The new man's name was Hughie, and his wife's name was June. They had come down from Aberdeenshire for the berry-picking, and were now looking for a place as winter quarters for a few months.

They had no kids as yet, and said they didn't want any. Jimmy and Lizzy felt sad for them not having any bairns. Wee Jimmy was the pride of their life.

"What do you do to make a living?" Jimmy asked him.

"Oh," he said, "I go dry hunting,[1] and so does the wife. Perth is no bad for dry hunting. Sometimes my wife reads the tea leaves. Aye, we make a fair livin, and we saved up at the berries as well. Now we are going to enjoy the money we saved. We are going to blow the lot on peeve.[2]"

Jimmy felt kind of edgy, because he didn't drink. Neither did

1. chapping at doors   2. drink

12

his wife. "Oh well, if they keep themselves tae themselves, it will be fine," he thought.

They didn't. They came home that night drunk and with a carry out of drink. They huddled round Jimmy's fire, and forced him to have a drink too. Lizzy was in bed, but June went and dragged her out of the bed and made her drink as well. They sat till all the drink was gone, and Jimmy and Lizzy just slept where they lay.

The next morning the two of them had the wildest hangovers ever, something they had never experienced before. They were sick all day. So Jimmy couldn't go to his poaching that day.

That night was the same. Drink never bothered Hughie or June, maybe because they were used to it, thought Jimmy. Again they came back with a load of drink. Jimmy and Lizzy, as I said at the beginning, weren't the full shilling, and were too feart to say no to them. So that night was a repeat of the night before – they got blootert.

This carried on for about two weeks, and Jimmy was getting a taste for it. After supper the next night, Hughie asked Jimmy if he had any money.

"Yes, I have a few pounds put by."

"Well, could I borrow a few pounds from you?"

"I will have to see if it is alright with Lizzy first."

When he went into the tent, Lizzy wasn't there. Wee Jimmy said she was away for the toilet. So Jimmy gave Hughie ten pounds.

He rushed away without even a backward glance. June came out of her tent and asked where Hughie was. Jimmy told her what had happened.

"So he is up to his old pranks again," June said. "Where is Lizzy, Jimmy?"

"She has gone for a sloosh.¹"

Well, they waited nearly all night, and neither Lizzy or Hughie never came back, and they never appeared all the next day as well.

1. pee

My father went over to see how they were getting on that Sunday. Jimmy cried when he saw my father. "Oh Biddly, my dear Lizzy has left me for another man – June's man!"

My father listened to what he had to say, sympathising with him.

"Well, Jimmy, there is only one thing for you to dae, take his wife."

Jimmy's head went up, and he looked at her.

"Are you game, June?"

"Oh, I might as well, one man's as good as another."

So that's what happened that year near Redgorton. Jimmy and June brought up wee Jimmy, and none of them ever put drink in their mouths again.

Through the Eyes of a
Tinker Child

When I was six years old, my mother and father said to me, "You must go to school, and learn to read and write like other bairns." So when the school started up after the summer holidays I was put to school.

I was a very shy child when I was six, and terrified on my first day. How would I be able to cope with spending time among the country hantle,[1] me being a traveller? I had never done it before. I had always been within the security blanket of my family. What was going to happen to me now?

In a state of panic, I held on tight to my mother's hand all the way down to the school. When we entered the school gates there were more kids than I had ever seen in my life before. So I crawled under my mother's coat like I used to do when it was cold in the winter. My mother hardly noticed what I was doing, as she was used to me doing it.

We went into the school through the front door, and were told to wait and see the Headmaster, a Mr Douglas. After about ten minutes, we were ushered into his office by the school secretary. A dour-faced woman, she looked frightened – of what, I was to find out later.

"Well," said the headmaster, "you want your child to go to this school?"

"Yes," said my mother, "I do, if it is alright with you." I burst out laughing. My mother used to make up little rhymes, and each line included the initial of someone's name. I said to her to complete the rhyme: "Somebody H is thinking of you".

1. non-travellers

At home we played games like this all the time. The headmaster glowered down into my small, impish face. "Well, we have a fine one here, a joker no less. We will soon put that nonsense out of you, my girl. You can go now," he said to my mother, "I will take her to her class."

My mother kissed me and told me to behave, not to cry, to do what I was told, and off she went. Mr Douglas took me by the hand to my class. He dragged me along as if I was a dog on a leash.

I went into the classroom and a smiling teacher greeted me with a cuddle. The headmaster said to the teacher, "Don't stand any nonsense from this one. She is one of the tinker-clan you know, and a bit of a joker, I believe."

"She will be fine with me, sir," said the teacher, and I was never so happy as when I saw this man close the door behind him. I got another cuddle from the teacher, and all my fears went away.

§

At playtime I was standing by myself in the playground eating a bit of toast my mother had made for me at the camp-fire that morning. I got pushed from the back and fell to the ground clutching my toast. A foot came down and stood on my hand with the toast in it, trampling my fingers and the toast into the ground.

I let out a yell, but soon stopped, remembering my granny's words: "The country hantle are always right, because they have the education, and we don't." I was brought up this way, to think I must have done something wrong that deserved punishment, and it was my fault that this had happened to me.

So I said nothing, and washed the mud off my hands, to make sure that the teacher wouldn't ask me what had happened. "The traveller is always wrong and they are always right," I kept saying that to myself all day.

When bell time came, I ran home as fast as I could. My sister was waiting for me at the school gate. Was I glad to see her, you bet I was. I never mentioned to anyone what had happened that day at school.

If someone was to ask me what was the worst memory of my life, it would be school, especially that first day.

§

For many days to follow, every evening I was pounced on by this same girl, who was called Morag. She was three times my size. The other children called her baby elephant. She used to lock me in the toilets and beat me up every evening. She would send me notes in class: "You are a TINK, and don't you forget it, scum." She used to sing to me: "Tinky, tinky, torin bags, Awa tae the well and wash yer rags!" Then she would slap me across the face, and she always stuck her own big fat face in mine. I remember saying to myself, if there ever were ogres, she was one of them.

A few days later she was off school. She must have been ill or something, and I was so happy not to be tormented for those few days at least.

While she was away, there was a new rule announced at school. We children would run and hang on the back of the milk van when the milk was delivered at playtime. The rule was that we were not allowed to do it any more.

However, Morag being off school didn't know this, so she jumped on the back of the van. She was sent for by the headmaster. He took her into her class, and using his double-thong belt, he strapped her in front of all the pupils in the room. I felt sorry for her, but not too sorry.

I remembered my granny's words at that time, "God's no sleeping." Were her words coming true, and was he protecting me?

One day Morag ripped the clothes off me, and sent me home in my knickers. I was mortified. She said I had been wearing her frock. How could I? I weighed about four stone, and she weighed about ten stone.

Her father owned a fruit shop. She used to bring rotten fruit to the school, and pelt all the kids in the yard with it.

One day she was caught kissing a boy behind a shed at school. The other children said they were "fumbling". At the time I didn't know what that meant. She was sent home with a note from the headmaster, and was off school for a week.

A few of the children got together and decided that when she came back we were going to do something about her bullying. I said I wanted nothing to do with it. So they left me out of it, but agreed that I could watch. That suited me fine. There were three boys and two girls that she always gave a hard time to. They went into the toilets, the boys in theirs, and the girls in theirs. The girls peed in a can, and the boys shit in a paper, and they waited and waited in one of the toilets all crushed together. I was waiting outside. She made a remark to me, but I have forgotten what it was, and went into the toilet. After about five minutes I heard this unearthly scream. The gang came out of the toilets so fast they nearly knocked me down. Then Morag came flying out, covered in pee and with shit running down her face.

At that very moment a teacher came round the corner, and saw her. The rest of us were chasing each other and playing away as if nothing had happened.

The teacher nearly took a fit when she saw her, and the smell was terrible. "Who did this to you?" the teacher demanded.

"I don't know, miss, I never saw their faces."

I can tell you, she still bullied us at school afterwards, but not so much. It was me she picked on the most. She blamed me for things I hadn't done. Then she went and told the teachers. I got the belt once while I was there. She plugged newspapers down the toilet and said I had done it. The headmaster sent for me, and I got the two-thong belt double handed. I never felt pain like that in my life.

When the headmaster told me to go back to my class, I ran home. Once my father saw the state of my hands, he took me with him and marched right into the headmaster's office. I was standing there terrified. My father grabbed the headmaster by the collar, took his two fingers and poked them into his eyes. "Will that fit you?" he said.

I was tortured at the school till I was twelve. Then I moved to the High School. I liked that a lot better.

Any travellers reading this will know what I went through at that time. I am now an old woman, yet that memory will be with me forever. But there's another thing you should always remember: "God's no' sleeping."

The Mistake

There was a funny thing happened to a cousin of mine at the berry-picking one year. He came out to pick my brother's berries, and he didn't have a partner. The way the work was done, two folk had to pick, one on each side of the drill.

Now, at the berry-picking at the same time there was another family who were a bit peculiar. They kept themselves to themselves, but if you went to their camp they made you more than welcome. Very nice people they were, but they didn't know much about the outside world, and how other people lived. They lived their life in a cocoon of their own making, and made their own rules.

The old man of the family had five daughters, and he was looking for husbands for them. We didn't know this at the time, so when we heard one of his girls didn't have a partner, my brother put my cousin with her.

Things were fine, till everybody had to weigh in their berries, and they all came down carrying their buckets. The girl's father saw her and my cousin come down to the bottom of the drill, and he was carrying her bucket of berries. He was just helping her out.

The father didn't see it like that. "You like my daughter?" he asked my cousin.

"Yes, she is a nice girl," he replied. It was the worst thing he could have said.

"Come up to my camp when you are ready," said the father, "and have a mouthful of tea."

My cousin Andrew said to me, "You are coming up with me, I am no' going up myself. I hear they are bad people, and very rough."

"OK, I will come up with you. I like them, in fact," was my reply.

My father was a man who liked a joke, and he asked us where we were going. We told him that we were invited up for a cup of tea. "Fine," he said, "I will come with you."

On the way up, my father was taking the mickey out of my cousin Andy. He told him he might get trapped into marrying one of the girls, probably the one he was picking berries with all day.

The look of shock on Andy's face was fear, pure fear. "I am only seventeen," said Andy. "I am no' wantin a wife."

"Well," my father said jokingly, "what were you doing in the bushes with her all day, then?"

"Honest tae my God, Uncle Alex, I never laid a finger on her!"

"Aye, but what did she tell her father, boy? That's the thing." My father had him nearly messing himself.

We got to the tent and they were all sitting round the fire. It took my father all his time to keep a straight face. It was like an Indian pow-wow, and believe me, they looked the part.

The old man murmured something to his wife in cant Gaelic, and we didn't hear what she said back, but she came out with a cup and saucer and handed it to Andy. The saucer was all chipped, and the cup wasn't in good shape either. I glanced over at my father, and he shrugged his shoulders at me. He was taken by surprise as well.

One of the girls came out and handed my father and me two mugs of tea. It looked like black treacle, and it was stewed with being on the fire all day. It tasted rank.

"Now," said the father, in a Highland accent (they came from up the north of Scotland), "you said you liked my girl."

My cousin Andy said, "I was only picking berries with her."

"That is good enough for me. Now we must plan the wedding. She has a dowry of ten shillings."

I couldn't keep it in any longer, I started to snigger. My father said, "Excuse Sheila – the berries always makes her do that."

Well, the three of us were dumbfounded. I whispered to my father, "What are we going to do now?"

"Shush," my father said, "I am thinking."

"Alright," said the old man, "I will tell you what I will do. I have never done this before, but I will peel the tent sticks for your bow tent, and they will be bonny and clean. Now there, you cannae refuse that, can you?"

Andy thought for a while, and said, "Well, I will have to go and tell my mother. She stays in Blairgowrie. I will be back in the morning."

The old man agreed, and Andy walked away waving to them, with myself and my father in tow. When he came to a place near the main road, my father said to him, "What are you going to do now?"

"I'll show you," he said, and he started to run like a whippet. He was gasping and sweating all the way.

That night he went to Montrose to stay with his sister. He married there and gave the berries a miss for a few years. But all that berry season, the old man and his sons were looking for him.

We will never forget the near-miss he had. It would have been the worst mistake of his life.

Poochie and Knot

Poochie was an old woman who stayed up near Aberfeldy. She was a very fat woman, and she lived with a man the travellers called Knot. Hence he was also known as Poochie's Knot. Poochie was always fat, and she blamed her mother for feeding her too much when she was younger. This was away back in the forties. They were travelling folk. They pitched their tent at Aberfeldy, and intended to stay there for as long as they could survive.

Now, what they did to make money was a very funny thing. They hawked the houses and farms, and when they got scrap or rags, they told the other travellers where it was, and the travellers paid them to be on the look out for stuff. They didn't make much out of it, but Poochie begged the houses for food and they just kept themselves alive.

One day they were walking through Aberfeldy when they met some other travellers. They stood speaking to them for a while, but Poochie was getting tired, and said she needed to sit down. "Well," said the other travelling man, "we will go down beside the wee burn wi' a couple screw-taps."

So down they went. It was a hot summer's day, and they were glad to get sitting down, especially Poochie. She lay there like a beached whale, and couldn't see anything past her belly. "Well, I got doon alright, but I'll never get up again!" she said.

They all started laughing. So did Poochie, and nearly choked herself, and what made it worse, her belly was wobbling like a jelly, and with her laughing so much, she was farting like a motor-bike. They were all in hysterics with laughter, and the more she laughed, the more she farted.

"Oh, oh, I need a sloosh[1] wi' all this laughing. Quick, help me up!"

No matter how hard they tried, they couldn't budge her. Knot started to shout at her, "You silly auld coo, how the hell did you get doon and cannae get up?"

"I don't ken how."

"Well, roll till you get on your belly. You might manage to get up then."

So she tried to roll, but it was no use. "Push me, push me!" she was shouting. So they pushed her, but the push was too hard, and she rolled down the bank into the river.

"I cannae swim!" she was shouting.

"Thikent[2] woman, it is shallow there, you can stand up!"

So she stood up, and relief came over her face.

"Are you alright, Poochie?"

"Yes, I am fine, but I'm no needin a sloosh ony mair, thank God. Get me oot o' here. I am soaking!"

They took her by the hands, and managed to get her up on to the bank of the river.

"Now, Poochie, don't lie doon, whatever you dae."

"I'm no that thickent to dae that again, Knot."

"Well," said the other travelling man, "I haven't laughed as much for a long, long time. Poochie, you have made our day. Come on, Belle, we will have to go now, it's getting late. Can we give you a lift to the camp?"

"Now, Alex, can you see me getting up onto that lorry? No way!"

Yes, the other traveller couple was my mother and father, Alex and Belle Stewart. They said they laughed all the way back to Blair.

1. pee 2. stupid

The Hedgehog

The Scottish travellers are so different in their ways, sometimes, to English travellers. Not all English travellers are different, but a family that came to the berries one year were unusual. I thought their habits were a wee bit strange, especially their eating habits. It was not so much their way of eating, but what they were eating.

The man of the family put up their tent, a bell tent. It was the first one of those I had ever seen. He made a fire and said to his son, "Get a heavy stick, son, and follow me."

The family had some girls as well, so I played with them while they were away.

The man would have been gone about an hour, and he came back with something in a bag. He lifted the heavy stick, felt the outside of the bag, and brought the stick down with a heavy blow. He repeated this three more times. Then he tipped out the contents of the bag, and there before us were four dead mankeepers.[1]

The wife washed them, gutted them and then just threw them on the greeshoch.[2] She was rubbing her hands and mumbling something. I couldn't understand what she was saying, but they all laughed. All I could catch of the conversation was something about "dinner tonight". I stared and stared at them – surely they weren't going to eat mankeepers! Well, not in front of me they wouldn't.

So I hurried home to our tent, and my mother had mince and tatties on the fire. I tried and tried to eat some of my dinner that night, but I kept seeing the eyes of the four animals looking at me. I couldn't swallow for the life of me that night.

1. lizards   2. cinders of the wood fire

I told my mother and father about it a couple of hours later, when I came to myself. "Well," my father said, "All folk are no' the same, Sheila, and you must respect that."

"Never," I said.

"The man asked me if there were any hedgehogs around here," my father added.

"What?" I said.

"Oh yes, it is supposed to be a delicacy, so he said anyway. If he catches one, I want you to watch how they cook it. You might learn something about other folk."

"Oh no, daddy, I cannae."

"Oh yes you will!" said my father.

The days passed, with me praying to God for them not to get a hedgehog. One day my father came to me and said a man out of another tent had got them a hedgehog. Oh dear no, I thought to myself, but I had to go to see how they cooked it, and explain to my mother and father how it was done.

So off I went down to their tent to watch. They were all sitting near the fire, and the man shouted to me to come in about. I knew then that my father had asked him to let me watch. I sat down on the grass as nervous as anything at what I was about to witness. My thoughts at that moment were that I wished I had been born a boy, they are not as feart as girls. Then I thought about having to stand up to do a pee, and I soon changed my mind.

The man went to where the earth was soft and filled a small bucket with it, and took it back to the fire. He shouted to the woman, and she brought the hedgehog from the tent. I couldn't tell if it was alive or not, because it was curled up in a ball. He put water into the bucket and mixed it with the soil until it was a thick clay. I was waiting for him to put it on the fire, but he didn't do that. He went away from the fire and dug a hole in the ground. He placed the clay all round the poor wee creature, stuck it in the hole and put the rest of the clay on top. It was completely covered. Then he took a shovel and started to carry the fire over to cover where the poor hedgehog was buried. He then made a big fire over it, and said to me, "When that fire dies out, the dinner will be ready."

I thought to myself, "You evil man! I hope you turn into a hedgehog, and let me catch you. I'll show you a hole alright – six feet under. You are not human." Of course I said nothing out loud as usual, but no one can hurt you for your thoughts.

I went to play with some of the girls at hide and seek, but all the while I kept glancing over to the fire to see if it was getting any smaller.

An hour later, the man shouted on me and the girls. We ran over to the fire that was nearly out now. He raked away the ashes, dug up the grave and took out the ball of clay that he had wrapped the poor wee thing in. The clay was peeled back off the hedgehog with a stick, and there it lay in all its glory. He lifted it, and starting from the tail pulled the skin upwards, and the spines came off like an overcoat.

I ran and ran, and when I got to our camp, as I was panting for breath, I looked at my mother so seriously and said, "Mother, don't ever let me marry an English traveller, will ye no'?".

I can't look at a poor wee hedgehog ever since that day. I couldn't have stayed to watch them eat it.

Folk Tales and Ghost Stories

❧

The Pig's Head

This short story was handed down to me by my family, and they swore it was true. I will leave it to the readers to make up their own mind.

Many, many years ago, there was a travelling family camping at the Hermitage near Dunkeld. They had three kids, one boy and two girls. The man's name was Willie and his wife's name was Jean, and she was expecting their fourth child. He was only twenty-eight, and Jean was twenty-six. They had run away from their families at an early age. They set up a bow tent of their own, a long way away, till the families accepted their relationship, which they did eventually. They came from Perthshire, and were glad to be back in their own shire.

They had settled in at the Hermitage to wait for the birth of the baby. It was the winter time and it was bitterly cold, but their gelly,[1] with a stove in the centre, was very cosy and warm.

Now it was always Jean, the wife, that hawked the houses and brought back the money. To earn this she drukkered.[2] But she was in no condition to do it at this time, so it was up to Willie to provide the habbin. He couldn't read palms, so he chapped on the doors to see if they needed any odd jobs done.

He did not too bad the first day – he made one shilling. That was a good lot of money in these days. It meant they had food for two days, because travellers always made big pots of what they call sloorich (something like an Irish stew). Everything available went into the pot, with plenty of potatoes. They were

1. double bow tent   2. read palms   3. food

28

very content that night with their bellies full, and enough left for the next day. (Even when I was growing up we only had one hot meal a day, in the evening, earlier we had tea and a piece.)

Willie started to tell the kids a story about what he had done that day, to get the one shilling. Parents were always telling stories to their children, especially about how to do their work. Willie did it so that the boy would learn how to look after his wife and family when he had one. Then he told the girls a story they would be interested in, till eventually the children fell asleep.

Willie and Jean decided that he didn't need to go out looking for work the next day, as they had enough food to last them two days. Willie was glad about that, because he had just about frozen that day doing odd jobs. But then he thought that he had a family to keep, and that he must not be lazy.

So the next day Willie goes out again to call on the houses for odd jobs, but he wasn't having much luck that day. Two pennies he got for sweeping a shop floor. With this he bought milk, bread and jam. At least the kids would have bread and jam to eat.

He happened to be passing a butcher's shop, so he thought he would go in to see if they had any scuddin' bits – leftovers that the butcher was chucking out.

"Come in," said the butcher. "I do have something I am throwing away. If you want it, you are welcome to it."

He reached under the counter and took out a pig's head, a big one it was. Willie's face lit up. "Thank you so much, sir, that would be grand."

Off he went back to the camp, and as he approached the bow tent, he walked more slowly. I will give them a fright, he thought, and make them jump. So he took a stick and poked it through the pig's neck. Then he lifted the flap and stuck the pig's head under the cover of the tent, making a pig sound.

Well, the screaming was deafening. First the kids came running out, then the mother, and Jean collapsed at Willie's feet with fear.

"It's only me playin wi' you," said Willie. Well, you should have heard the tonguing he got from Jean and the kids. He was laughing hard, but soon stopped when he saw the state they were in.

The next day they cooked the pig's head, and it lasted them a couple of days.

A week later, about three in the afternoon, Jean took her pains. Now in those days, doctors or midwives wouldn't attend a traveller's confinement. So the day before, they had taken the three kids down to Perth to stay with Jean's mother until the baby was born.

When Jean took her pains, it was up to Willie to be there to help her, as he had done once before. They didn't have to wait long for results. The baby was born.

Willie was struck dumb as he looked at the child he held in his arms. He looked at it, and it had a piglet's face. "Oh my God," he thought.

"Let me see my child," Jean cried. "Is it a boy or a girl?" He held the baby up to let her see it – it was a boy.

When Jean saw him she started screaming. "Why? Why?" she was shouting at Willie. Without a thought, Willie lifted up the flap of the tent and threw the baby out into the cold snow.

"What have you done, man? It is our child. Go and get him."

Willie went out and brought the baby in, and cleaned the snow off him. When he looked down, it was a normal baby. The two parents cried and cried. All was well.

"It was the auld Ruffy,[1]" said Willie.

1. Devil

The Skull

There was once a young minister who had just finished at college, and he was sent to a parish to start his ministry. The old minister was retiring soon, but he stayed on for a few weeks to show the young man the ropes and introduce him to the folk of the parish. Then the old minister retired, and the young minister was left on his own.

The only thing that bothered him about his ministry was writing his sermons for the Sunday. However, he found a place that was peaceful and it helped him to concentrate – a graveyard.

One day he was walking round the graveyard when he came across a skull. He stared at it for a long time, and said out loud, "Oh my God, skull, but you have beautiful teeth. I have never seen any so white."

"Thank you," said the skull.

The young man was very shocked when he heard the skull speak. "You can speak, skull?" said he.

"Yes, I can," was the answer.

So they started up a conversation, and it lasted about two hours.

"Well," said the young minister, "I must go now, but that was a wonderful conversation. It was the best one I have had since I arrived here. Can we meet and talk again? I'll tell you what – after church next Sunday, will you come to my house for tea, about three o'clock?"

"I will," said the skull. So the young minister left it at that.

All that week, the young minister couldn't wait till he saw the skull again so he could have a decent conversation.

At two-thirty on the Sunday, the young man told his house-keeper he was having a friend to tea at three o'clock. The housekeeper set the table with scones, and lots of other good things to eat.

At three sharp the young minister told the housekeeper to look out of the window and see if anything was coming. "No," said the old woman, "I see nothing."

The young man was getting very agitated. Surely the skull will come, he thought. "Look again and see if you see anything coming," he repeated.

She stared out of the window. "Well, I see something coming, but it looks like a turnip rolling down to the door."

"You are dismissed for the day," the minister replied.

He ran to open the door, lifted the skull into his house, and put it on the table.

"You carry on and have your meal," said the skull. "You can appreciate the food. I cannot eat, but you have your tea and we can have a chat."

So the conversation went on for two hours. Then the skull said he had to go. "Well," said the young minister, "again that was a great conversation. When can we meet again?"

"What about next Sunday?" said the skull. "But this time, you come to me."

Eagerly the young man agreed. "Where can I find you?"

"You know where you met me that first time, at the back of the church. Down at the far end of the graveyard you will find an avenue, and there I'll be. But remember this: you must come on your horse, and whatever you see on the road you must ignore, and don't interfere."

The young minister said he would follow the skull's instructions to the letter.

The next Sunday afternoon he had the horse all ready waiting for him, and at the appointed time he made his way down to find the avenue. It was strange that he had not noticed it before.

Thinking of the great conversation he was going to have, he cantered on. He came to a quarry where there were two men digging sand and putting it into a barrow that had no bottom to it. He thought this was very strange, but carried on. Going through his mind was the skull's voice, saying not to interfere.

Another mile down the road, he came to a small cottage. There was a woman standing at the door with her mouth wide open, and rats and mice were running out of the cottage and into her mouth. "My goodness," thought the young minister, "that is terrible."

He kept riding down the road, and a mile further on he came to another wee cottage. Standing at the door was a young girl, who had an old woman by the hair, and was beating her severely with a stick. "Oh dear," thought the young man. "That is the worst one yet."

He moved on again until finally he came to a house, and there at the door was the skull.

"Good afternoon, your Reverence," said the skull.

"The same to you," said the young man. Then inside the house he went, and there was the table set for tea.

"Do help yourself, minister – you know I don't eat."

They started to chat away, and it was, as always, great conversation. They talked till the minister said that he had to go home.

"Wait a minute," said the skull. "Are you not curious about the things you saw when you were coming down the road?"

"Well," said the minister, "I thought it was none of my business, so I didn't ask."

"Well, I am going to tell you. When you came down the road, the first thing you saw was two men shovelling sand into a bottomless barrow, did you not?"

"Yes, I did, and I thought it very strange, but I said nothing and carried on."

"Good man," said the skull. "Well, that was a parable. In fact it is right that they have to do this, the reason being that they worked on a Sunday, and this is their punishment. They have to keep on doing it for eternity. Now," said the skull, "the next thing you saw was the woman standing at her door, and the rats and mice running in and out of her mouth."

"Yes," said the young man, "I also wondered about that one."

"Again," the skull said, "it was a parable. That woman had a small croft, with one cow and a few hens. One day a tinker girl came to her door, and asked her for some milk because the baby was hungry, and gave the woman a penny. The woman grabbed the bottle and the penny, and went through the room to the dairy. When she had gone in there, she saw that in one of the basins of milk was a drowned mouse. 'This is good enough for tinkers,' she thought. She filled the bottle with the milk that the mouse had drowned in. A few days later the baby died with a disease that it got from the milk. So she has to stand there for eternity as her punishment. The third parable was the young girl beating the old woman with a stick."

"Yes," said the minister, "I was curious about that one too."

"That young girl was an orphan. One day she passed the old woman's house, and stopped to ask her for a drink of water. She got the drink, but then the old woman tied her up with chains around her ankles, so that she couldn't run away. She beat the girl to death. So, for all eternity, the old woman has to be beaten by the girl."

The young minister felt that there was something wrong here, and began to be very uncomfortable. "I must go now, skull, thank you for your kindness."

"Wait a minute," said the skull. "How long do you think you have been here?"

"Oh, about two hours," replied the minister.

"You have been here two centuries. When you go up the avenue, you will see iron birds fly in the sky, and iron beasts running on rails, and many, many things you will not be familiar with. So take this blanket and put it over your horse's saddle, and when you reach town don't step on the ground without first throwing down the blanket to stand on. Now away with you."

The young minister spurred his horse into a gallop to get away from the skull, and headed for home.

34

Suddenly he heard a tremendous noise, and sure enough there was an iron bird flying overhead. Then he saw many, many things he was not familiar with, including houses built up high, one on top of the other.

He became frightened, and this turned to anger when he got into the centre of town. The noise was unbearable. In his anger he sprang off his horse without putting down the blanket first, and he went up in a puff of smoke.

The Keeper of Life

There was, once upon a time, an old man who was the keeper of life. That was his job, every day. He would go to this big brick building, open the huge door with a special key, and go inside.

Inside this building there were thousands of candles, all lit up. The ones he found not lit were of people who had died. He would start all over again and light new ones for the births.

He had tried for many years to tell his daughter to pick a nice sensible man to marry, one he could rely on to take over his job as the keeper of life. But every man she brought home wasn't suitable.

One day he went to his work as usual, and he said to himself, "I must look at my own candle today, and see how it is getting on." When he arrived, he went straight to his own candle. "My god," he thought, "it is getting very small." So he cut a bit off one of the other longer candles and stuck it on his one to make it bigger.

That night his daughter brought another young man home to meet her father and mother. He was the nicest young man anyone could ever meet. The old man was so happy and excited. "At last I have someone to take over my job for me," he thought, "and let me retire."

So he asked the young man if he wanted the job, so that he could retire.

"Yes," said the young man, "I would be grateful for the job." The old man said he would teach him the job the next morning.

The keeper went to his job that day, humming to himself. He was in a jolly mood. When he got to the door of his work, he opened it and went inside. It had always preyed on his mind about the candle he had made shorter, so that he could have a longer life. He went up to the candle he had cut, and he found out, to his horror, it was his daughter's candle he had taken the bit off. Panicking, he cut his own candle and put the bit back to the way it was.

Next morning, and for the next week, he showed the young man the job. At the end of the week the young man said to him, "What are you going to do now, as this is your last day?"

"Well, for the years I have left, I am going to do what I have always wanted to do – I am going to be a *storyteller*."

The Wooden Ball

There once was a carpenter, and people said he was the best in the land, but he had one problem. Before he died, it was his greatest ambition to meet the King.

He thought long and hard about it, and one day he came to his wife and said, "I am going into my workshop. Do not disturb me, as I might be there for a few days. I will come out when I am ready." The wife agreed.

He was in there for three days, and his wife was getting worried about him. Finally he came out of the workshop, and he had a square box in his hand.

"What do you think of that?" he asked his wife.

She took the box in her hands and said, "It is beautiful."

"No, no," said the carpenter, "look inside the box." So she opened the box, and looked inside, and she took out a ball.

"Oh my goodness," said his wife, "this is so beautiful." It was made of all kinds of wood, cokobolla, ebony, African redwood, white wood. Ivory, diamonds, mother-of-pearl and many more precious stones were set in it. It was so lovely, it felt as if it was jumping in her hand, and the stream of light it gave off was like a rainbow.

"Do you think," said the carpenter, "it is fit for a king?"

"Oh yes," said his wife. "Indeed it is."

Off the carpenter went to the Palace. He knocked on the door, and a butler came out. "I have come here to see the King," said the carpenter. "I have a special present for him, but I must deliver it myself."

"Wait there," the butler said, and went inside. He came back a few minutes later, and showed the carpenter into the King's throne room, where the King sat on his throne. The delighted carpenter could not believe it. Here was his monarch, and he was standing before him. This was his life's ambition.

He bowed and said, "I have a special present for you, sire, and I had to deliver it myself." So he handed the King the box.

"Thank you," said the King, and the carpenter left the throne room, bowing all the way out.

The King studied the beautiful box, then he opened it. He took out the wooden ball, and oh my goodness, the light that came out of it was nearly blinding. He studied it, and it felt as if the ball was moving in his hands, and the lights of the rainbow were dancing like stars on the ceiling. "I have never seen any thing this exquisite in my life," said the King.

As he stared at the ball, his eye noticed an inscription on the middle of the ball. It said, "Pass this on to the one you love best."

"Oh," said the King, "well, the one I love best is my old dog, and I can't give it to a dog. I suppose I will give it to the Queen."

Off he went to the Queen's chambers and knocked on the door. The Queen came to the door, and the King said, "I have a special present for you, my love. It is only fit for a queen, and I am giving it to you." He thought hopefully she would let him enter, but no, she took the box, said "Thank you," and closed the door in his face.

She sat on her bed and opened the box, put her hand in and took out the ball. Looking at the beauty of the ball made her tremble. The lights that came from it took her breath away. She had never seen any thing so lovely in her life. Then her eyes caught the inscription: "Pass this on to the one you love the best."

"Well," she said. "The one I love best is the captain of the guard. I will give it to him."

She hurried to the captain of the guard's chamber, and knocked on the door. He answered it, and she said to him, "My love, I have a special present for you. It is only fit for a king, and I am giving it to you." He ushered her in, and she was in there for about two hours. Then she left.

When she had gone, he sat on the bed, picked up the box, and opened it. He took out the ball, and it sparkled like nothing he had ever seen before. He had to hold it with both hands, because it was jumping prettily in his grasp, and the rainbow lights were amazing to see. They lit up the whole room, in many colours. Then his eyes caught the inscription, "Pass this on to the one you love best."

"Oh," he said, "Now let me think. That young scullery maid that started last week, a pretty little thing, I will give it to her. Then that will keep me in good stead with her. Yes, that's what I will do."

Off he went to the kitchen, and the scullery maid was just finishing her chores. "My dear, I have a special present for you. It is only fit for a queen, but I am giving it to you."

"Just put it on the table, I must get this kitchen finished," said the scullery maid. So he left it on the table, bowed to her, and departed.

When she had finished her work, she picked up the box, and ran to her bedroom in the loft. She was tired out. She looked at the box, and was so in wonderment of it, she threw it on to the bed. She gazed at it for a long, long time. Then she lifted it and took out the ball. Her two eyes nearly popped out of their sockets. She had never seen such beauty in her life, and never knew that some of the colours that shone from it ever existed. Her hands trembled at the feel of it. She examined it, and saw the inscription inside: "Pass this on to the one you love best."

She thought for a while, then said to herself, "Well, the one I love best is our monarch. I will give it to him."

Off she went to the King's chamber, and knocked on the door. The King opened it. She said, "Your Majesty, I have a special present for you, one that is only fit for a King," and she handed him the box, bowed and left.

He closed the door and looked at the box. Then he said, "I should have given it to my bloody dog in the first place."

Johnny, Pay Me for My Story

Once upon a time there was a widow woman and her son. They lived on an island far away from everyone. The laddie used to get odd jobs here and there all over the country, and when he came home at night, he was that tired he just went away to his bed.

One night he was just going to bed when there was a knock on the door. "I wonder who this can be at this time o' night?" he said to his mother.

"You better go and see," she said, "you never ken who it could be."

So Johnny went to the door and opened it and peered nervously out into the darkness. There was an old man standing there. "I am lost," he said. "I just saw your light and wondered if you could give me shelter for the night."

"Come in," said Johnny. "There's naebody bides here but me and my auld mither."

So he took the old man in, and his mother made him a cup of tea and a bite to eat, and they sat talking at the fire. Johnny said, "You must travel far, what do you do for a livin?"

"Well," said the old man, "I am a storyteller".

"Ah," said Johnny, "that is the very thing I wish for every night, that someone would come and tell me a story."

"Would you like a story, laddie?" asked the old man.

"I would be very glad o' a story just to pass the time."

So the old man started to tell them a story.

Once upon a time there was a king miles and miles from here. He was a good king to all his subjects, and he had four lovely daughters. Also this king had a miller, who had four sons.

One day, when things were very quiet, the four sons went away looking for work for themselves. They were strong young men and could get work anywhere.

They travelled on for days and days, till they came to a cross-roads. The oldest one said, "There's no use us going together looking for work. We will split up, and we will meet here in a year and a day."

They all agreed to do this, and they each took a different road. The eldest one was a big strong intelligent man, and he went along asking for work, until he came to a big house. He knocked on the door, and a gentleman came out.

"Well, my boy, what do you want?"

"Well, sir, I am looking for work," said the eldest son. "I am willing to do anything."

"Come in, come in, and have some supper," said the gentleman.

So in he goes, and the man is asking him questions. "Are you sure you are willing to try anything?"

"Oh yes, I am," said the boy.

"Well, I am what you would call a star-gazer, and I have been looking for a long time for a mate, to teach him the things I know."

"Oh," said the oldest brother, "that is the very thing for me." So he stayed with the gentleman and learned the star-gazing business.

Now, the second brother searched and searched for a job, but couldn't get one. Eventually he came to an awful rough-looking house. He rapped on the door, thinking to himself, "I don't think there will be much work here."

The door opened and a very rough-looking man came out. "What the hell are you doing here at this time of night?" he asked.

"I am looking for work," said the lad. "I will work at anything."

"Would you do anything for money?"

"Yes, I would do anything."

"Well," said the man, "you're the very man I am looking for, I am a professional burglar, and I would like an accomplice, one that I can trust and show the tricks of the trade to, so if you would like to stay with me, you could earn yourself a lot of money."

So that was the second brother got a job.

The third brother was coming along the road, and he came to a castle where people were shooting with bows and arrows. "I will go down there and ask for a job," he said to himself.

So he sat in a bush till most of the folk were away, then went up to the front door. Out came a gentleman and asked what he wanted. "I am looking for a job," he said. "I will do anything you want me to do."

"Oh," said the gentleman, "come in, and I will teach you a good job, if you want to try it. I'll teach you to be an archer, the finest archer in the world, and you can win a lot of prizes."

"Oh," said the boy, "that would be fine. I will just stay here, then."

Finally, the youngest brother was coming along the road. He wasn't as big and strong as the rest of them, and no one took him on for a job.

At last he came to a wee old house, and he rapped on the door. A wee old man opened it. "What do you want, son, at this time of night?"

"I am on the road looking for a job."

"Oh, there's no' much work here," said the old man, "but come in and you'll get a drop of tea, and I will share what's in the house wi you."

So the boy goes in and sits down, and he says to the old man, "You won't be working any mair, you're too auld."

"I am too auld for work now, son,", he replied, "but I used to be the best tailor in the whole district."

"Oh, I wish I could do that," said the laddie.

"I will teach you to do that, son," said the old man, "if you

43

want to be a tailor." The young man agreed, and stayed with the old man, and started his apprenticeship as a tailor.

Time wore on, till it came to the day the four brothers had to go home.

The four of them all met together at the crossroads. They shook hands, overjoyed to see each other, and asked each other about the trades they had learned.

But when they came back to the mill, their mother and father were dead and gone. So the four brothers went up to see the king.

"Hello," said the king, "have you had your breakfast?"

"No," said the oldest brother. "There is nothing to eat at the mill."

So the king took them in and gave them a first-class breakfast, then he took them out to the back of the castle. "Now," he said to the oldest brother, "I have a task for you. You are a star-gazer, you tell me: You see that nest in the bourach[1] of that tree?"

"Yes," said the oldest brother, "I see it."

"Well," said the king. "Tell me how many eggs are in that nest, and I will give you one of my daughters to marry."

"There are four eggs in that nest, sir," said the star-gazer.

The butler went away and got a ladder, and climbed the tree and looked into the nest. "There are four eggs in it, sir," said the butler.

Then the king turned to the brother who was the thief. "Now, I want to see you go up and steal an egg from that nest, without disturbing the bird. If you can do that, you can have my second daughter's hand in marriage."

The thief went round the tree, and round the tree. He climbed up the tree, and stole an egg from under the bird without the bird moving. He turned, and held the egg up between his fingers and his thumb.

The king said to the archer, "Now, I want you to crack the shell of that egg with an arrow without bursting the yolk.

1. cluster of branches

If you can do that, you can have my third daughter's hand in marriage."

"Oh, but that is an easy thing for me to do," said the archer. He took his bow and arrow and took aim, and just tipped the shell with the arrow, so that it cracked in two shares in his brother's hand, without bursting the yolk.

"Well," said the king to the youngest brother, "it is your turn now. See if you can sew the egg back together so that it is the way it was."

"I will do that," said the youngest brother. So he got the finest needle he had, and his brother came out of the tree and handed him the egg. He sewed it with the very fine needle and very fine thread, and you couldn't see the crack in it at all. The thief put the egg back in the nest under the bird, without disturbing it.

"Well," said the king, "you are all clever men. There's no getting away from that. You each have won your brides, and a farm each, and when I die, all my estate will be split in four. Come back in the morning and we will arrange for the marriages to take place."

The four of them went back to the mill as happy as can be, and enjoyed laughing and joking all night.

They went up to the castle first thing in the morning, and they found the king and queen wringing their hands, and the princesses tearing their hair out.

"What's wrong?" they asked. "What's the matter?"

"When we got up this morning, our youngest daughter wasn't in her room, and there's no sign of a struggle there, and the window was torn out of the frame."

"Wait a minute," said the star-gazer. "I will tell you where she is, and what has happened to her." He studied for a while, then said, "I ken where she is."

"Thank God," said the king.

"She is alive, but she's in bad hands," said the star-gazer. "Out in the fresh-water loch there's a castle, and there's a warlock bides there. He came last night and stole your daughter, and she is locked up in that castle."

45

"Oh," said the king, "what are we going to do now?"

"If we can get a boat," said the star-gazer, "we have a good chance of going to get her."

The king got them a boat, and the brothers set off. They sailed through a blanket of fog until they reached an island where a big old dreich castle stood in the middle of a wood.

"Now," said the eldest brother, "this is where she is, and there's only one man can do anything for her, and that's you." He pointed to his brother the thief. "If you can get her out and back to the boat, we've got it made, but remember, that's a warlock in there, and if he gets you, it will be death for you."

Out went the thief, slipping quietly up to the castle, and he made his way silently through the rooms, till finally he came to the room the princess was in. In no time he had her out of the room and down the stairs.

Just as he got her back to the boat, the warlock woke up from his sleep, and discovered the princess was away. The boat was making good speed, with the wind behind it, but when they looked back they saw a black cloud coming through the air. When it got near, it was the warlock, looking like a giant black bat, and he swooped at the boat with his talons.

The archer managed to keep him off, with an arrow here and there. But then the warlock made a dive at the boat, and tore it in half.

"Oh," said the tailor, "I'll need to sew this up quick!" So he sewed it up while the others manned the oars. The archer waited for the right moment, and he fired an arrow that went right through the warlock's throat, and he fell dead in the loch.

They managed to get to the shore, shaking and sore, and the water running out of them.

The old king was delighted to get his daughter back. "That was very well done," he said. He took them inside, and they got dry clothes, and the weddings went ahead, and they are still living happily to this day.

"Now," said the old man to Johnny, "What do you think of that?"

"Oh," said Johnny, "that was very good. That was the best story I have heard for years." "Well," said the old man, "I am glad you liked it, for that's my trade. Every story I tell, I get paid for it."

"Oh well," said Johnny, "that's a different kettle of fish. I have no money to pay anybody." "In that case," said the old man, "you will have to pay a forfeit."

"What have I got to dae?" asked Johnny.

"I'm going to turn you into a lion," said the old man, "and I am going to send you out into the woods for a year and a day. When you come back, we'll see if you can pay me for my story then or not."

So the old man turned him into a lion, and he went away through the woods for a year and a day, leaving his old mother in the cottage by herself.

When the year and a day was up, Johnny came back in the gloaming dark, and his mother was sitting at the door greeting. He had turned back into himself again, and she said, "Oh Johnny, Johnny, I'm glad you're back!"

She hurried to make him a bite to eat, and then he went to lie down because he was so fatigued.

It had turned dark when a knock came to the door again. "Who could that be at this time?" said Johnny, but when he opened the door, there was the same old man again.

"Oh," said Johnny, "it's you again."

"Yes," said the old man. "It's me again".

"We haven't got much in the house," said Johnny, "because you ken where I was for a year and a day."

"Yes," said the old man, "and now, Johnny, you can turn yourself into a lion any time you want."

"Oh, thanks very much," said Johnny.

"Now," said the old man, "are you going to pay me for my story?"

"Where am I going to get money, wandering in the wood in winter, with frost and snow?" asked Johnny.

"Oh well," said the old man, "I will have to turn you into something else."

"Can you no' have mercy on me?" said Johnny.

"It's for your own good," said the old man. "I think I will turn you into a salmon, and give you a change in the sea for a while."

So Johnny was off down to the river side, where he turned into a salmon, and he was away to the sea for a year and a day. Then instinct brought him back to the burn, and like a flash he turned back into a man again on the bank.

All that was wrong with him was that his feet were damp, because it was a shallow bit of the river he had come into. So he wandered over to his house where his mother was sitting waiting for him to come back.

"Ah, Johnny," she said, "you have come back, son."

"Yes, mother, I have got back. It was a cold carry-on for me spending winter in the sea. I got chased by otters, chased by seals, chased by sea lions. Everything possible I have been chased by. I was near gaffed twice by fishermen."

"Oh well, you are hame noo, get some dry clothes on and have a wee bite to eat."

Johnny changed into dry clothes, and got a wee bit of supper, and he was just sitting talking to his mother, how she was and how she had survived while he was away for the last year.

Then a knock came to the door again. "I bet you a shilling, mother, it's that man back again, and if he asks this time for money, I have nothing, not even a penny."

So when he opened the door, he saw the wee man standing there again.

"Aye," he says. "You're back again, Johnny. Am I getting in this time?"

"Oh yes," said Johnny, "you can come in, you're just as welcome the night as you were two years ago."

So the old man came in and sat down at the fire. He asked

Johnny how he got on in the sea. So Johnny told him how many times he was in danger with otters and seals, and many more underwater animals. Johnny told him everything.

"Oh, you are a clever boy, Johnny," said the old man, "but I am not going to be here long tonight, I have another appointment someplace else, and I have just come back to see if you're going to pay me for my story."

"Ah, there is no use saying things like that," said Johnny. "You ken fine I would get no money in the sea."

"Oh, I'm sorry for you," said the old man, "but I am going to have to give you another forfeit till you come to your senses. You've been a lion, and you got on very well in the wood, and you got on all right as a salmon in the sea. This time I will give you a chance in the sky. I will turn you into a hawk. It might come in useful to you afterwards."

Just like that, Johnny turned into a hawk, and soared up into the sky away above the woods, and he could see right across the sea.

"Ah, this is better," says Johnny. "Nobody will chase me up here."

He was flying away here and there, and he went further away this time than ever he went before. With just a pull at his wings he could sheer away up in seconds and come back down again.

That year as a hawk wasn't so bad, and when Johnny was on his way back he thought, "I will rest here in this wee sheltered spot, and I will manage hame tomorrow night some time." He looked and he saw a wee house in the middle of a wood. It was surrounded by ivy bushes, and ivy grew up its walls.

Johnny flew in and sat on the window sill underneath this ivy. It was a great shelter, and he could hear everything that was going on in the cottage through the window. There was a man and a woman and a lump of a boy, an awful cheery boy, laughing and having fun with his mother and father.

Johnny heard someone coming to the house, and when he looked, it was an old man, the same old man that had come to him. The old man knocked on their door, and the folk opened the door for him and took him in. He got his tea and his supper. Then the boy asked the old man to tell him a story. So the old man told him the same story he had told Johnny. Johnny was sitting at the window with his ears cocked to hear what the boy would say, after the old man finished his story.

"Well," said the old man, "That is the end of my story. When I tell a story I expect to be paid for it, so what are you going to pay me for my story?"

"Well, I haven't any money," said the boy, "and I can't pay you, but maybe God will pay you."

"That's fair enough," said the old man. "That will just suit me fine! You can go scot-free. If you hadn't said God would pay me, I would have given you a forfeit. But you managed to be sensible in your words, and you said the right thing. So I bid you good night." And away the old man went.

"Well," thought Johnny, "if I had just thought of that reply I would have been a free man. I know what to do tomorrow when I get back to my house."

As soon as daylight came, Johnny made back to his own house, and as he neared his house he couldn't see any smoke coming out of the chimney, or any movement about the place. As soon as he had turned from a hawk to himself again, he went into the house, and there was nobody there. There was no sign of his mother, and the place was bare and empty.

He kindled up a wee fire and then he searched the place from top to bottom. All that was in the house was a bed and a few old blankets. He just had the fire going great when there was a knock came to the door. It was the old man again. "Ah," said Johnny, "you're back!"

"Yes," said the old man, "I am back, Johnny. I have sad news for you. Your mother died six months ago. That long cold winter she couldn't look after herself. But I buried her. I gave her a good down-putting, a very expensive funeral."

"Oh well," said Johnny, "That was very kind of you."

"Well, Johnny, you know what I am back for."

"You are back for the payment for your story," said Johnny.

"That's right," said the old man. "Are you going to pay me for my story?"

"Well, it's just like this, old man," said Johnny. "I can't pay you, but maybe God will pay you."

"Ah, that's well chosen," said the old man. "If you had said that a few years ago, you would have been a free man. But that's three things you were turned into, the lion, the salmon and the hawk. You can turn yourself into any of them when you want to. I think that is not a bad prize."

"Thanks very much, old man," said Johnny, "but there is nothing for me here now, so I will be moving on. I'll need to find some work, some other place to make a living."

"Well," the old man said, "away along the coast there is a big house, and there is a man there and he is looking for a man to pick the right horses, and you might get a job there."

"Fair enough," said Johnny, and away he goes in the direction the old man told him. It was two or three days travel, and he was about half a mile from the big house when he heard a voice calling. "Hi! Come here, Johnny, help!"

Johnny looked up into a very tall tree, and away at the very top he saw a man sitting. "There is a man stuck up that tree," says Johnny, "and he will be wanting me to go for a ladder."

"Come closer to the tree," the man said. "Would you no' like to come up here? I can see the whole world from where I am."

"Oh no," said Johnny, "that's a thing I never got used to, climbing, and in any case, I am too tired to climb away up there."

"It's dead easy," said the man. "Come closer to the tree."

Johnny took two steps closer to the tree, and before you could say Jock Robertson, he was up at the top of the tree beside the man.

"Well, what am I going to do up here?", said Johnny.

"Look away over there," said the man. "You will see a big house over there." And with that the man disappeared, and Johnny was stuck up at the top of the tree. Johnny thought to himself, maybe he is away for a ladder, and sure enough about an hour later the man came back with a huge ladder, and Johnny came down.

"Now," said Johnny, "what was all that about?"

"I have been waiting on you, Johnny," said the man.

"How do you know my name?"

"Oh, fine I know your name," said the man. "You'd better come with me to the castle, and I will tell you what I want you for."

Away the two of them went to the castle, and Johnny got his supper.

"I know a lot about you," the man said to Johnny. "I have a half-brother, a bad evil man, and he lives across the loch there. He came at night and stole the only daughter I had. I want you to go and search for her and bring her back to me."

"Oh, I could never do that," says Johnny. "Why can you no go yourself?"

"I can't go myself," said the man. "I haven't got the powers you have. I'll get you a boat, and I will get you men to sail it. You go and try and get my daughter back for me. If you do, the castle will be yours and you will have my daughter's hand in marriage."

"Fair enough," said Johnny, "I will try anything once."

It was arranged that Johnny got the great big sailing ship, men to sail it and a captain to guide it.

"Now, before you go there," said the man, "I will tell you this. My daughter can't get freed till my brother dies. I can tell you that there will be three things he will say that will end his life, and once he says the third one he is gone."

Johnny sailed away in the boat and sailed for a long time. The captain was a first-class captain, and he navigated the ship in the direction the man had told him. Early one morning, one of the mates came down to tell Johnny he was wanted on deck.

Up Johnny went, and the captain said to him, "Do you see that island over there? That's where the Laird's daughter is. His half-brother is a warlock, and can put a curse on you".

"Oh, can he?" said Johnny. "We'll see about that."

When they came within about five or six miles of the island, Johnny said, "We won't go any closer. Stop here, and wait for me." The captain lowered the anchor, and Johnny jumped overboard, turned into a salmon, and was swimming for the shore. He came ashore about half a mile from the castle, and he turned himself into a man again.

He stood up and looked around him, and walked along the beach. As far as he could see in every direction, he saw a great big wall. He ran back a bit, then turned himself into a lion, and over the wall he jumped. Once he was in the estate, when he looked around and could see no one, he turned himself into a man again so he would not frighten anyone by being a lion. But when he came closer to the house he saw a lot of big dogs, so he turned himself in to a hawk, and flew from tree to tree.

When he came to the castle he flew round it, and started going from window to window looking in. Finally he came to a window where he saw the girl inside crying her eyes out and tearing at her hair. He sat on the window-sill till she saw him, and she came forward, lifted the window up a bit and let the wee hawk into the room. "Ma poor wee bird," she said, "you must be cold sittin' out in that rain."

The minute Johnny got inside the room, he turned himself back into a man again. "Oh my God," she said, "what are you, who are you?"

He told her all he had been through, and she said, "You met my father?"

"Yes," he replied, "and he gave me a lot of instructions. He said that you would never be free until the warlock is dead."

"That's right," she said, "and I don't know how in the world he is going to die, for he is so fly that he can't be tricked."

"Well, ask him tonight how he is going to die," said Johnny.

Johnny then turned back into a hawk again, and he sat at the window-sill. He could see out over the sea. He saw a sailing ship coming into a jetty, and a great big man coming straight up to the castle. "I bet that's him," he thought. "I hope she gets the right answer."

Up the big man came, and sure enough it was the evil warlock. He was coming up to the girl's room to make sure she was still there. "I am still here," she said. "It's been a long, wearisome day. I haven't had much pleasure out of it. I wish I was at home."

"Oh, you will get home alright when I die," said the big man.

"When you die?" she said. "When will that be?"

"Do you see that hump of ground out there?" said the man. There was a green knowe outside the castle with trees beside it. "When the wee birds carry it away to build their nests in other places and the hump becomes level, that will be the end of my life."

The next day the warlock went away again, and Johnny came in. "Well, what did he tell you?" he asked.

"He said when that knowe gets taken away by the wee birds to build their nests, that would be the end of his life."

"You go out," said Johnny, "and chase all the birds away with a big stick, and see what happens."

So out she goes with a big stick and chases all the birds away. When the warlock came back, he said to her, "What are you doing, my dear?"

"Oh, I am chasing all the birds away because they are taking all the mould off the knowe. I care for your life more than anything in this world."

"Oh, I am sorry, my dear," said the warlock. "I was telling you a lie. That's not my life at all. You see that big stone there? It used to be a big stone shaped like a horse, with four big legs sticking out of its long body. When that melts away and the fog grows, and covers all that stone, that will be the end of my life."

So the man went away, but he didn't go right away, he just went down out of sight and hid. The girl went to get buckets of water and a scrubbing brush, and started to wash the stone and polish it. The man thought to himself, "The girl must be fond of me, right enough."

He wandered back again. "I see you have made a fine job of that stone, but I am sorry to disappoint you, for that's not my life at all."

"Well, what is your life, then?" she asked.

"I'll tell you," he said. "There is a log of wood down on the beach and it's sixteen feet long and five feet thick. There must be a man to split that log with one blow of an axe. Out of the log will come a wild duck, and it will fly right across the sea, and when it is high up in the heavens it will drop an egg, and that egg must be broken on my brow where this mark is," and he pointed to a circle on his forehead. "That will be the end of my life."

Johnny was listening to all this, and said to himself, "That is the third thing, and the girl's father told me the third thing was the right one. That's it."

Johnny flew back to the boat as quickly as he could, and said to the captain, "Have you got an axe on the boat?" The captain got out a great big axe. Johnny sharpened it, and sharpened it, and sharpened it, till it was like a lance. Then he went back with it to the castle.

The next morning, bright and early, once the warlock was away, Johnny said to the girl, "Get yourself ready and come with me." When she had gathered everything together she went away with Johnny.

Soon they came to the big high wall. Johnny turned into a hawk, flew right over the wall and landed on the shore where the men were waiting with a rowing boat. "You will have to go back to the ship again and get a big rope," he told them. So they went back to the ship and brought back a big rope.

"Stand along the side of the wall," said Johnny, "and catch the rope when I give it from the other side."

Johnny flew back over the wall, and turned himself into a man again so that he could fling the rope over. He said to the girl, "I will tie the rope around your waist, and the men will pull you over the wall, but you will have to help them by climbing yourself." It was no bother, however, she just walked up the wall and down the other side as easy as anything.

"Now," he said, "where is this big lump of wood he was talking about?" He walked along the shore till he came to it. Then he lifted the big axe, and split the big log the way you would split a cabbage with a gully knife, and this wee wild duck shot right up into the air.

Johnny turned himself into a hawk again, and he went up after the duck. He was crowding it, and circling it, and with the fright this wee duck was getting, it dropped an egg from the air. Johnny came low down to the water, turned himself into a salmon, and went after the egg. He took it in his mouth, got out of the water, and turned himself back into a man again.

Then they spotted a sailing ship speeding towards them. "Oh," said the girl, "That's my uncle coming!"

"Get into the boat all of you," said Johnny. They got into the boat, and pulled hard on the oars towards their big ship as quick as ever they could, and they finally managed to get on to the ship. But, oh me, the warlock drew alongside, and he was seething with anger. He had a sword seven feet long, and he came off his own boat and onto their boat.

Johnny was waiting for him, and he ran up to him and hit him with the egg right on the brow. He fell on his back stone dead.

So Johnny and the girl were married and lived happy ever after.

This was a story that was in my family. It is an ancient old story.

Heather Meg

This story goes back maybe a hundred and fifty years.

There was a travelling woman who was camped in the Sma' Glen near Crieff. They called her Heather Meg, because she sold heather on the streets of Crieff, at Crieff Games and at all the shows that were held there. She was a wee small creature, but she could always make a living to support herself.

One day she was selling heather as usual at the Games, and as she was walking down the street counting her money that she kept in a wee pouch, she was attacked by two men who worked on a farm in the area. They pounced on her and grabbed the bag of money. Then they gave her a beating. When she came to herself, she headed for the police station.

The policeman said to her, "Could you recognise the men who did it?"

"Yes," she said, she could.

So they took her out to the street again, and she pointed out the two men who had robbed her. They were taken to the police station for questioning. However, when the police asked them if they had robbed wee Meg, the men turned it round about, and said it was she who had stolen their money. That's why they had given her a beating, and had taken the money back from her.

Of course the men were believed, and poor wee Meg was thrown in jail, into an underground cell. She asked the policemen for a drink of water, to drink with a smoked trout she had brought for her dinner, but they said no. She was locked up on her own, and started to eat her fish as she had nothing to eat all day, and was hungry.

She had eaten half of the fish, when she started to choke on a fish bone. She hammered and hammered on the cell door, but no one came. Early the next morning the police came down the stairs to see Meg, and they found her dead. She had choked to death on the fish bone.

Years had passed since wee Meg's death, but there were strange things going on in the police station. Policemen saw at various times an apparition on the stairs going down to the cells. One policeman saw a figure walk out of the wall of the office. The cells were pretty full one night, and they put a farmhand into the cell that Meg had died in. When they went to get him out in the morning, he was dead. His two eyes were sitting on his cheek, and there were marks on his neck, big black-and-blue marks made by a small pair of hands. Many years later this happened again to a ploughman from another of the farms.

So they decided to brick up that cell, and never to use it again. It was bricked up two days later, but the ghost was still there. One day the sergeant of police was sitting at his desk, when he felt a breeze of wind passing him. He looked round, and he saw a drawer open on its own, with no one there. He went over to the drawer and took out a paper he found there. On this paper was written the truth about what happened to Meg by one of the men who had robbed and beat her up, and this proved her innocence.

The police sergeant went for the priest, and he blessed wee Meg, and threw holy water all around, and prayed her soul would go to heaven. From that day on there was no further disturbance in that police station, but they kept the cell bricked up.

The Funeral

This is a story I got from an old man the other side of Forfar. It happened many years ago, and he swore it was true.

There was a traveller woman died between Forfar and Montrose. She wasn't a really old woman, maybe in her forties. They were camped in a wee wood, and when her man got up one morning, he found her dead. She wasn't a great wife – a bit snappy at times.

They had one daughter, she would be about twenty years of age. When the father told the young girl her mother was dead, she started to cry, sobbing her heart out, and shouting, "I wish God had taken me instead of my mither."

There was no pacifying her at all, and she kept repeating the same words over and over. So her father just left her to get all her crying over and done with, then she would feel a bit better. She was holding her mother's hand, and cradling her in her arms.

"I am sad too, daughter, but there is nothing we can do about it," said her father.

"There must be something we can do," said the girl, "to bring her back."

"Don't be thickent.[1] You ken better than that – once you're deid, you're deid, and you can never come back. I thought you had more sense than that, lass."

"I am sorry, Da, but I wasn't thinking straight for a minute."

"That's alright, lass. I ken how you feel. Losing yer Ma like that must have been an awfy shock for you."

1. silly

59

She smiled and looked at him, and said, "At least I still have you, Da."

The man went down to report the death to the police. That's what travellers did in those days, they went to the feekies (police). The girl stayed with her mother, speaking to her, while her dad went to report it. About an hour later a horse and cart pulled up to take the body away and put it in the police mortuary.

"Will we be able to see her again before the burial? Could you leave the coffin open for the relatives to pay their last respects?" asked the man.

"We don't normally, but this time we will, if you ask us to. Usually we just bury you tinks the same day they die."

"Well, I am asking you, don't put the lid on the coffin till we have all seen her."

"Alright," said the feekie.

The man got in touch with his relatives, and his wife's relatives, and told them when the funeral was to be. It was a pauper's funeral of course, because he had no money, and she would be laid to rest in a pauper's grave.

The day before the funeral was the day the police said they could view the remains, so all the travellers who wanted to see her were there. The girl went to her father and said, "Can I be last to go in Da, before they put the lid on?"

"Surely, my lassie, you can. I will go in just before you, then you can go in last."

"Thanks, father, I would like that."

There were a lot of family wanting to see her before she was laid to rest. It was now the turn of the father to go in. He was about ten minutes saying his last goodbyes.

Then the last one was the girl. She went in with a wee smile on her face, eager to see her mother again. She talked to her for a long time. Then she bent down to kiss her goodbye. But when she was finished kissing her, and lifted her head, it wasn't the girl but the mother who was standing there. The girl was in the coffin.

The mother hid her face and said to the police, "You can put the lid on it now, I am finished." She walked out of the door to where everyone was standing, and some of them started to scream. It was the mother, not the girl, that came out of the door.

The father rushed back into the room, and as he came in they had just nailed the lid on the coffin. "Open it again!" shouted the father.

"But we have just nailed it down."

"For God's sake, man, do as I ask! I wouldn't ask you if it wasn't important."

The relatives crowded into the room, and watched the policeman take the lid off the coffin. Lying there was the young girl, and not her mother.

How this came about no one was able to tell, but the wife lived for a long time after that, and the daughter certainly was dead. There was a hearing about the case, but no one could shed any light on it at all.

There are more strange things in life than we can ever imagine.

The Pilgrims of the Mist

This story happened up at a place they called Cock Mist in Perthshire. My granny told me this one.

Long, long ago there were some travellers who were frightened of the mist. They thought it was God being angry with them.

A family arrived one day about the month of September, and said they were going to stay in the glen for a while. Their name was Stewart. The day was a wee bit nippy, but the sun was shining. They pitched their tents on a nice flat bit of ground.

There were three tents, for Granny and Granda, their son and his wife, and their six bairns. They had been down at Blair picking berries all summer, and were ready for a rest now. They decided they might stay for a few weeks in the glen. It was nice and quiet, nobody to bother them. They went to bed that night a very contented family.

The old man got up in the morning, kindled the fire, and had the can boiling for his old wife when she got out of bed. She made the tea, of course – the men never did that.

They were sitting eating a lump of bread and cheese when they heard the rest of the camp stirring. The old woman had refilled the can for the others getting up. "Come on, Betsy, or the can will be aff the boil!" she shouted to her daughter. Her daughter crawled out of the tent.

"You look like a ferret getting oot among straw. Take it oot o' your hair."

"Too bad aboot ferrets and straw. I am mouded[1] for a sup o' tea. I cannae get Geordie to move this morning at a'."

1. dying

"Och, leave him alane for a while yet, he has nothing to rise for."

The bairn came out of the tent next. "Mammy, mammy, I slooshed[1] mysel, and I'm a' scaddit.[2]"

"Come here, my wain, and granny will sort you."

The bairn ran to her granny, and she put a dry pair of knickers on her. Then her mammy gave her a bit of bread and cheese.

"That's good cheese, mammy."

"Aye, I got it fae the farm on the way up here. It's just newly made."

"My daddy will like it tae."

"I am bad aboot thick-lippet Geordie. If he doesn't get oot o' that bed soon, he won't get any."

"I hear you misca'ing me, woman!" Geordie shouted from the tent.

He crawled out of the tent next, made a grab for the can to get his tea, and tore at the bread and cheese and stuffed it in his mouth. "That's better," he said, tickling his wife under the chin.

"Awa wi' you, thick lip, or should I call you scabby heid?"

"I cannae help it if my heid got cut crawling through the wood getting sticks."

"I will kiss it better, Daddy," said the bairn.

"Better no', you might get parries[3] in your mooth."

"Awa'," said Geordie, "I'm no parriefied."

"Well, what was that that bit me last night, then?"

"You can guarantee it was nae parry."

"Shut up, ye fool, the bairn's there."

It was another hour before everyone was out of bed, and then Geordie had to spread the straw out to dry, because the lassie had slooshed on it.

Once they all were fed, Granda said to his son, "Come on, we will hae a walk in the woods and see if we can feek[4] any moochies[5] for wir habbin[6] the night," and off they went with some snares to set.

1. peed 2. sore (on the bottom) 3. lice 4. get 5. rabbits
6. our food

They came back about two hours later with three rabbits. Rabbits were a staple diet for the travellers in these days, and hares as well. They gutted the rabbits and skinned them and put the three in the pot, and made rabbit stew and tatties.

There was a wee stream beside them, and they were living life to the full. They had a horse named Dan, and they would go down to Alyth to the shops for what they needed.

They had been there for about a week when what they feared happened. The men were away rabbiting through the woods, and the women were doing their washing. All of a sudden a mist came down, and it was as thick as pea soup. The woman got terrified, grabbed the bairns and made into the tent. They were saying to themselves, "God, what have we done to deserve this?" In their own humble way they thought God had done it to them.

The fog lasted about five hours, and they stayed in the tent all that time, clinging to their children. After the mist cleared they waited for the men to come back, but there was no sign of them. They made some tea and sat round the fire. But it grew dark, and still no sign of the men.

Next morning they heard shouting: "We are here, women!"

The women and children scrambled out of the tents, and welcomed their men back.

"My God almighty, what happened to you two men?"

"Oh, dinnae ask. That mist came doon and we could see nothing. Geordie here stepped into a bog up to his knees, and I was all night holding his hand so that I wouldn't lose him, and to keep him being sucked in further. I never in my life saw such mist, we couldn't see wir finger in front o' us, but it cleared up. I was petrified. I got Geordie oot o' the bog, and we ran hame, thank God. Are you women and the wains alright?"

"Aye, we are fine noo that you've come back."

"We are leaving this place," said the old father. "Get packed up now, we are no' meant to be here."

So they all packed up, and when they were ready to go, they sat on the cart and the old horse pulled away. They made for Alyth, and decided they would stay on the show green.

When they got to Alyth and pitched their tents, there were two other families on the green, travellers they knew.

"Hello there, Geordie, where you been hiding? I haven't seen you since last berry time, and you missed the berries this year. Where were you?"

"I saw you, Willie, this year at the berries."

"No, no, that was last year, Geordie."

They all stared at Willie in disbelief. "What year is it then?" asked Geordie.

"It is 1892, exactly a year ago to the day I saw you last."

They didn't say much to that, but went into their tent and they all sat round. "We have lost a year," said Geordie. "How and why I don't know, but dinnae mention it again. Tell no one but wir ain family."

That family of travellers were known as "The Pilgrims of the Mist" among the Stewart clan.

The Buttons

This is a story told to me by a gypsy woman who used to have a showground. The shows is what we called them, but other people called them the fair. It was a woman at the shows who pierced my ears. Her mother told me this story, and it was about her mother.

This is something that happened to her mother before they had the showground. She told fortunes, and was a medium as well. When she was about thirty, she went around the houses chapping at the doors, selling lucky charms, and telling fortunes. She went to a big house one day, and the lady brought her in. She sold her two lucky charms, one for the lady, and one for her mother who was in hospital. Then the lady said, "Wait there a moment, I have something else I would like to give you. Sit down, I won't be long."

She came back in ten minutes with a beautiful coat. "Take this. I am sure you will find some use for it, and I think it will just fit you. I have put weight on and it doesn't fit me any more, and you are quite welcome to it."

The gypsy thanked her for it, and thought to herself, "This is the most beautiful coat I have ever seen in my life." It was made out of soft velvet, but it was lined, and the buttons on it were round silver ones – six down the front of the coat, and one on each sleeve at the cuff. The colour was black, but the silver buttons showed it up perfectly.

The woman was so proud of this coat, she wore it every day. One day she was walking down the street in Dundee, selling her lucky charms. Then a man came up to her while she was eating a roll. He grabbed her and took the coat off her back. She was screaming blue murder, but no one came to help. The man made off with the coat. "You thief!" she called after him. "You will have no luck from this day on, for stealing my good coat."

"Awa' ye silly bitch!" he shouted back at her.

She knew well enough there was no use going to the police, they wouldn't do anything. Not for a traveller, anyway. Very sad, she went home that day, and thought, "My lovely coat, it's gone."

A few months later, another show woman told her there was a man looking for her. "What kind o' man?" she asked.

"An ordinary-looking man with no heels on his shoes. He had a mark on his cheek. It looked like a birth blemish, a big one."

"I don't know anyone with that description."

"Oh, he said he will be back tonight."

"Ah well, let him come."

She went into her wagon to make her man's tea. An hour later, there was a knock on the wagon door. Her man opened it, and there stood a man, asking to speak to the gypsy's wife. Out she came, and she recognised him from the description she got from the other gypsy woman. The big blemish stood out.

"Well," he said to her, "I am the man who took the coat off you in Dundee that day. Please, please, take the curse off me. My wife put the coat on, and the buttons burst into flames, every single one of them. She was severely burnt, and look at my face, trying to save her. Please take the spell off me."

She took him into her wagon, and said something to him. He went away a happy man. What she said, I don't know, I wasn't told.

The Ghost in the Tent

This story came from an old travelling man I tracked down in Fife. It happened many years ago to a family he knew very well. He camped beside them often. One night as they sat round the fire they told him a story about a ghost in the tent.

About five years earlier, they had pitched their tent on the shores of Loch Fyne. There were other travellers there as well as them, travellers they knew.

After they put their tent up, one of the other travelling men came to them and said, "I wouldn't pitch your tent there, if I were you. That bit of ground is haunted."

"Away wi' you," replied the man of the family, whose name was Danny. 'I don't believe in ghosts. I am fine where I am."

The traveller man shrugged his shoulders and walked away, shaking his head.

All was well. They had their tea and they were relaxing round the fire, when Danny's wife, Maggie, said to him, "What if it is haunted, Danny?"

"Oh, awa' wi' you woman, of course it's no' haunted. We picked a good place to pitch our tent, maybe they were keeping this spot for somebody they ken. Don't be silly, woman, give me another cup of tea, make it a bit stronger this time."

Maggie said no more, but she was a bit eerie.[1]

Nothing happened that first night, they all slept like logs. Next morning they got up, kindled the fire for their tea and had their breakfast, before they went hawking. They hawked all day, selling their wares and drukkering.[2] It was about four o'clock when they got back to the tent site.

1. frightened   2. reading palms

Danny and Maggie had a boy and a girl. The boy was three, and the wee girl was one – they were too young to understand about ghosts.

They had their tea that night, and a blether round the fire with the rest of the travellers, and downed a couple of drinks. The kids were in bed, sound asleep, and it was now getting late. So they decided it was bedtime for them too. With the drink in them they fell asleep quickly.

About three in the morning, two hands gripped Danny round the ankles, and he woke up. The hands felt very clammy and started to drag him out of the bed. He was sliding down the bed, and was nearly dragged right out of their tent, but Maggie awoke, grabbed him to pull him back and managed to save him.

Danny jumped out of bed, and made round to the outside of the tent where he was being dragged, but there was no one there. He decided he would wait till morning, when perhaps he would see footprints. He thought maybe it was a joke the other travellers had played on him. If they had he would soon put them in their place, joke or no joke.

Morning came and Danny went round to the side of the tent to look for footprints, but there weren't any. The ground was as smooth as silk. This puzzled him somewhat. He thought maybe they had been smoothed out, after the ones who attacked him had gone.

No one in the camp said a word that day to Danny, except to acknowledge good morning with a nod. "That's funny," thought Danny. "I thought they would be gloating this morning after their scary trick." But no, everyone went about their business as usual.

Danny didn't say anything to the other travellers, but when they were on their own, he said to his wife, Maggie, "Maybe it was the peeve[1] we had last night, and we were dreaming?"

"Both of us?" replied Maggie. "I think not. I was frightened, and so was you, wee man."

1. drink

Danny let it drop for the time being and they went hawking again.

"If anything happens the night, we are moving in the morning," said Danny. It was a long dreary day, but they weren't in a hurry to get back to the tent. Danny could still feel the clammy hands round his ankles, and shivered every time the thought came over him.

That night when they got back, all the other travellers were there. "Well, Danny, you were a long time the day, you must have done well."

"Aye, no' too bad," said Danny.

They had their food for the night as usual, and the kids went to sleep in the tent. Maggie and Danny didn't want to go to bed. They were the last to go to bed that night, but they wanted to be in beside their bairns, so they crawled in. They were a good while in bed before they finally dropped off.

They awoke with a start. There was a horrible face staring into theirs, a woman with her hair all tousled, and grinning like a banshee. They were frozen like stone, and covered their heads till morning. The next day when they got up, their hair was as white as snow. They packed up and never went back to that campsite ever again.

The Girl at the Gothans

This is a story I collected from an old man in Thurso. He was about eighty-nine at the time, but a strong-willed traveller. I spent three days up there during the year 2007, with the greatest character I met in my story-collecting experience. He was one of the old-time travellers of a bygone age. He started his story, and the words just flew out of his mouth, as if the story had happened yesterday.

When I was a young man about twenty, my family always went down to Blairgowrie, to the berry-picking, and we always stayed at the Gothans. There were a lot of travellers there for the picking, and me being a young strapping man, I was looking for other things as well, in the shape of girls.

We picked every day, because my family needed the money, and you weren't allowed to stay on the ground if you weren't picking the raspberries. When the day was over, that's when the blackguarding (having fun) started – chatting up the girls, and I was first in the queue, getting my twopence worth in.

Honest, Sheila, it was great times. All gone now, worse luck, but at my age now I wouldn't be able to keep up with the young ones.

Now to get back to my story. We lived down at the bottom of the Gothans, and I had to walk back every night when I left my fellow travellers, my pals as they would say today.

One night I was walking to where my tent was, on a clear moonlight night, when I saw a girl coming towards me. I said, "Hello, there," and she turned to face me and said, "Hello. My name is Jenny, what's yours?"

"I am Colin. You are very late on the road tonight, Jenny," I said.

"I am having my walk. I am too busy all day to do it, so I walk at night."

"Where do you live, then – nearby?"

"Oh yes, in one of the cotter houses just up the road."

Now, to describe this lass is a bit difficult. Oh, not her looks, but there was something about her. I just couldn't put my finger on it, for the life of me.

She had blood-red hair that wasn't long. In fact it was cut close to her scalp like they did in the moich canes[1] to stop neets and parries.[2] I couldn't see the colour of her eyes, but they looked big and bulging out of her head. She was a pretty girl in a way. She was dressed in a tartan skirt and a white blouse.

"Are you not cold?" I asked her.

"Me, I'm never cold. Will you be here tomorrow night?" she asked.

"I might be."

"Good," she replied, "I will see you about eleven, the same time as tonight."

"Can I see you home, Jenny? It's lonely going up the road yourself."

"Indeed you can not," she said abruptly. She walked away, then turned around and said, "Tomorrow night, remember," and was gone out of sight.

I thought about her all day, wondering why she was such a strange girl, I thought to myself, each to his own, she was maybe strange, but this made me all the more determined to see her again, to find out more about her.

We had fun at the berries the next day, we all had a berry fight in the field, and got hell from the gaffer. He threatened he was going to sack us, but of course he was only kidding. He was a good man really.

The young boys asked me if I wanted to go into the town, Blairgowrie, after my supper. "Aye, I think I will," I said, and off we headed, walking to Blair. I will never forget that night, that's when I met my wife Susie, who I married a few years later.

1. mental asylums   2. head-lice

72

Susie was like a rosy apple, that's the only way I can describe her. We hit it off straight away, and I was to meet her the next night.

She was staying at the Ponfaulds, but the travellers called it the Ponfads. It was after twelve when I got home that night, and I had forgotten all about Jenny. When I got to my tent I remembered her, and went to the road and looked for her, but it was too dark to see anything. So I went to bed thinking about my wee Susie, with her rosy red cheeks.

Things went fine for a few days, but one night Susie said she was going home to see how her granny was, as she had fallen and hurt herself. So I wasn't seeing her that night.

At about ten that evening we were sitting round the fire with a lot of travellers, telling ghost stories, and one of the men said, "Did you ken this place is haunted?" Our ears sprang up, and three of us said, all at once. "By what, by who, where?"

"Oh, she walks along the road, past the tents, every night."

"Ah, you're telling lies," said Geordie, my pal.

"No, I am not. She was going with a traveller boy who was here picking berries, and her father found oot. They lived in a wee cotter hoose up the road. Her father took her and cut all the hair aff her head, then whipped her senseless, and in a few days she died. Now, what was her name again?" – and he shouted to his wife who was in the tent, "Maggy, what was the name o' that lassie that haunts this place, I've forgotten."

She shouted back, "Jenny was her name, Jenny Duff."

"Aye, that was it."

I looked at them sitting there and I could feel my face going white, and a tremble went through my body.

The next year we went to the Ponfads, and never went back to the Gothans again, and I never told a living soul till now.

Twa Sisters

I heard this story from a young woman up north. Her mother used to tell her it, and swore it was true.

On the top of a hill away up in Sutherlandshire was a gelly[1] and in this gelly lived two sisters. They had never married, for the simple reason that they had loved the same man, but he went away with another woman many years ago.

They lived as sour-faced women, deprived of life, as they thought. The horrible thing about these sisters was they never spoke to each other. They lived in the same tent, but each made her own food, and they had their own beds and did their own hawking. The oldest one's name was Sarah, and the other was Mary. Sarah was about forty-five, and Mary about forty-two.

One day other travellers came with their horses and carts and said they wanted to winter there on the hill. They chose a spot lower down and pulled on. There were six tents.

Now the two sisters never had had anyone stay beside them before. These travellers were Irish, and had not long come off the boat. Sarah came down the hill to speak to them, to say it was her and her sister's camping ground, and they were not allowed on it.

A big burly-looking Irish woman answered her, with such a heavy thick Irish accent that Sarah didn't know what she was saying, but she could see the woman was not happy about the way she had spoken to her. She went over to one of the men, and asked, "Could you tell me what the woman said to me?"

"Yes, I can," he said. "She said for you to go away and not bother her, but not quite in those words." He smiled to the

1. bow tent

74

other man who was holding up the tent, until the stones were laid on the sides to keep the tent down.

Sarah said she was not afraid of any long, dirty-tongued Irishwoman – this was her country, and she was the boss of her own campsite.

"Do you want to face her up, sure?" asked one of the men.

"Fight, you mean? No way, I would kill her if I got started." She headed back up the hill, and disappeared into her tent, saying no more.

Now Mary was away hawking when the Irish travellers came to the site, and when she came home, she knew Sarah wouldn't be pleased at their arrival. She was a more of an outgoing woman, and liked company, except for Sarah's. She often wondered to herself why, in all these years since their mother and father died, they had never buried the hatchet and spoken. But the way Sarah went on, she would rather bury the hatchet in her sister's head.

Mary went down to the travellers and welcomed them to the site. She only did this to upset Sarah. Sitting at her fire she had made outside the tent, she was watching every move Mary made, and fine Mary knew that. The Irishwoman spoke to Mary very civilly. She spoke slow so that Mary knew what she was saying, because her man had told her they didn't understand her speech.

Now Sarah and Mary, although they never spoke to each other, were a devious pair. They were not nice women at all. The folk of the town nearby were terrified of them, and called them witches.

Two days later a few of the Irish travellers moved on, and there was only one family left. They had one son, who would be about in his thirties. Sarah always stared at him when she saw him, and thought to herself, he looks like a tasty morsel. So did Mary.

They both knew what the other was thinking. Mary said to herself, "I will have him first."

She followed the lad into the wood one day and had her way with him, and this continued for a few weeks. It was always at night. When Mary was hawking through the day, Sarah followed him and had him as well in the daytime.

As the weeks passed, the two women became more content. They both fell with child, but neither realised that the other one had had the boy as well.

When the mother and father found out about this they were so angry at the women enticing their son to badness, as the mother called it. She went down on her knees and prayed to the Lord God above, in the name of the Virgin Mary, to put a curse on both of them and their unborn children.

They then moved away the next day. Before they left, the Irish woman left two bits of cloth, tied in a knot, and fastened to two separate trees. Her husband asked her why she did this. "Because those knots I have tied are the two babies' souls, which will stay on these trees. When they rot the babies will die. They won't have long lives." The man shook his head, and they moved on.

Well, the time came for the babies to be born. Mary had twins: both were born blind and deaf. Sarah had a wee girl, and she was born deformed.

The children lasted a few years, then died. Mary died first, a few years later, and Sarah lived till she was eighty. She was evil till the day she died, and she and her sister Mary never spoke ever again.

The Shearer

This is a story that happened many years ago. It starts in Blairgowrie and ends in Glenshee. It is a story that should not be forgotten; the travellers that tell it say it is the God's honest truth.

Many, many years ago there was a young man came to Blairgowrie to do the berry-picking. He worked all the season, six weeks, and made a lot of friends at the camp where he was staying. He was a very nice young man, about twenty-three years of age.

When the berry season was over, his friends knew he had saved up all the money he had earned, and so they enticed him to the pub, where they drank and drank. He stayed longer in Blairgowrie than he intended, until all his money was gone and so were his friends.

He woke up one morning and said to himself, "I must go away from here and head up the glen to look for work for the winter."

Late that afternoon he started walking up by Glenshee, on the road to Braemar. He walked for a while and a wind blew up, and it started to snow heavily, and it was dark. He thought to himself, "I should have left earlier. I can't even see the road in front of me." But he ploughed on. He was frozen half to death, and couldn't stop shivering. Then he noticed a light away in the distance to his right. "Thank God," he thought to himself. "At last a house." So he headed for the light.

When he arrived at the place it was a cottage, and through the window he could see a big fire burning in the grate. So he knocked on the door, and an old man answered it, saying. "My God, son, what are you doing here on a night like this? Come in, man, and get a heat at the fire." The young man took off his coat and hat and shook the snow off them, and went into the cottage.

"Sit down, son, and get a bowl of soup to warm you up," said the old man's wife. He was given a big bowl of broth, but before he had it he was so cold he couldn't even speak. After he finished his soup, he started to tell them why he was in the glen, and that he had been down picking berries in Blair and he was looking for work for the winter.

"Well, I haven't much work because I only have a small croft and I can manage it myself. What's your name, son?" asked the old man.

"John, John Stewart," replied the young man.

The old man thought deeply, and then said to him, "Well, John, I will tell you what I will do. We have a shed at the bottom of the garden, it has a bed in it, and a wee queen stove. It is very comfortable. You can sleep in there, and you can stay if you help me with the chores. I cannae pay you, but you will be fed, and have a roof over your head till the snow goes away."

"Oh thank you," said John. "That will be great. Just the thing."

So John moved into the shed to sleep. He was a great worker, and the old man had nothing to do.

The old man and woman got very fond of the young man, and treated him like a son. They had never had any children of their own, and they felt happier than they had been in years.

Spring arrived, and John helped with the lambing, both in Glenshee and in Glen Isla. He did the lambing in Glen Isla, and every one of the farmers got to be very fond of him. He was a great worker, and he got paid for what he did.

Now the shearing came around, and the old man said he would teach him to shear the sheep. Once the old man's sheep were sheared, he and the young man would help the Glen Isla farmers, and they would get paid for it.

By the time they had finished their own sheep, John was a great shearer. For every sheep the old man sheared, John sheared three. He took to the shearing like a duck to water, and he loved it. He was the best shearer in Glenshee and Glen Isla, and everyone thought the world of him.

John stayed up Glenshee for a couple of years, working in the glen with the old man and the Glen Isla boys. He had a good bundle of notes saved up, but he was too happy to move on from the glens.

One day he came to the old man, who now looked on him as a son, and asked him if he could take the old dog for a walk up the glen. "Of course you can, son. Away you go and enjoy yourself on your day off." So John headed up the glen with a smile on his face – he loved it up there.

Time wore on that day, and in the afternoon the rain came bucketing down. At five o'clock the Shearer, as the glen folk called him, wasn't back. The old man and his wife were getting worried, when ten o'clock came and still there was no sign of him, or of the old dog. The old man made several trips to the shed, but he wasn't there.

The old couple sat up part of the night, but the Shearer never came home. When the old man awoke the next morning about five o'clock, he ran down to the shed to see if he had returned, and there he was in his bed. "Thank God, son, you are home!" He touched him, but he was soaking with sweat, and couldn't speak.

The old man shouted for his wife to come and sit with him, till he went for the doctor on his horse. He came back with the doctor, and they waited outside the shed door while the doctor was examining him.

When the doctor came out he was shaking his head, and had a worried look on his face. "I am sorry to tell you, but he has double pneumonia, and he won't last the night. The only thing you can do is to make him comfortable. He got soaked when he was out, and slept with his wet clothes on, and they have dried on him."

They were in a terrible state, and sat up beside his bed through the night. At three in the morning, the Shearer died.

Word got to Glen Isla very fast, and the mourning started for the Shearer.

The day of the funeral came and all the Glenshee boys were ready to carry the coffin up to the graveyard. The graveyard was situated near the crossroads that led to Glen Isla, and when they got there all the boys from Glen Isla were standing at the crossroads with big clubs in their hands. They said to the folk from Glenshee, "He was as much our shearer as he was yours, so we want him buried in Glen Isla." The Glenshee boys objected, of course, and said he was being buried in Glenshee.

A fight started, and they were knocking lumps out of each other. There was an awful battle going on, and blood everywhere. Then all of a sudden it was as if someone had pulled a black curtain over the sky, and everything became pitch black. There were no birds whistling, all was silent.

The men stopped fighting, and in fear they waited. The darkness lasted a few minutes, then it was as if the black curtain was pulled back, and daylight came through, and the sun was shining, and when they looked down where the coffin had been, there were two coffins there.

They looked at one another, and the Glenshee boys picked up one coffin, and the Glen Isla boys picked up the other one, and one was buried in Glenshee, and the other was buried in Glen Isla. To this day no one knows where the Shearer is really buried.

Tales of Love and Loss

✸

It Wasn't To Be

There was a traveller lassie called Mary, though her family called her Trixy for a pet name. Her age was about sixteen or thereabout. She wasn't a bonny girl, but she was attractive, because she was always smiling and cheery. Her family lived away up in the east coast of Scotland, but travelled in the summer to find agricultural work. They went all over.

It was about 1902 this whole thing happened. They were camped at a farm, and were harvesting the farmer's neeps.[1]

Trixy's father, Wuggie, wouldn't let her use a huke,[2] so Trixy stayed at home and cleaned up the camp and made the food for them coming home from work. She also had to go up to the farm for milk and tatties, because in these days if you worked to a farmer you would get these things free, but they had to be collected every day.

However, this day, as Trixy went to collect the provisions from the farm, the farmer's wife wasn't in. Trixy went all round the farm looking for her and shouting her name. As she was passing the byre where the cows were, she heard a voice shouting, "In here."

So she went into the byre, and this young man was milking a cow.

"What you doing?" asked Trixy.

"I am milking a cow, can't you see, fool," he replied without looking up at her.

1. turnips   2. a knife for topping the turnips

"Oh I thought you had to pump its tail to get the milk," she said, and she burst out laughing.

The boy stood up and they saw each other for the first time. They were both laughing so loud the cow started to kick back with fright, and spilled the milk. This made them laugh all the more.

When they stopped laughing, a figure appeared at the shed door. It was the farmer's wife.

"Well, what's going on here, with all this laughter? I haven't heard laughter like that for a long, long time."

The boy spoke up and told her about pumping the cow's tail to get the milk out. Then they all laughed.

Trixy got her can of milk, and her boiling of tatties. Now, that was a meal to a traveller long ago. Tatties and a bowl of milk. The boy told her his name was Bobby, and helped her to carry the tatties and milk down to the camp.

She was going up to the farm for a few days after that, but Bobby was nowhere to be seen. She shrugged her shoulders and said to herself, "Oh well!"

A few days later, her mother, who was called Susie, took sick, and Trixy didn't know what to do. There was no use going for a doctor, he wouldn't come to tinkers. So she went up to the woman at the farm to see if she could help.

The farmer's wife was more than happy to go down to the camp and see her mother. On the way down, she told Trixy that Bobby was away to Aberdeenshire to collect a bull, with his father the farmer, and it would be about a week before they were back.

They got to the tent. The woman went inside and told Trixy to stay outside. Fifteen minutes later she came out with a smile on her face.

"She's alright, she is with child! You will be having a wee brother or sister."

"Oh my goodness, oh my goodness," Trixy kept repeating to herself. "Wait till Daddy and my two brothers hear this news." She thought to herself it must be a wee girl. She wanted a sister.

There was great enjoyment that night at the camp. They bought a bottle of whisky to celebrate which they all drank except Trixy. They had a great time singing and dancing round the fire.

It was a different story the next morning, because they couldn't get up for work. The farmer came down, as he had heard the news, and congratulated them.

"Don't bother working today, lads, you all look kind of delicate this morning. How many rows did you shaw this week?" (A row was four drills.)

"Five rows."

"Well, if you come up to the farm later I will pay you for that, seeing it is Friday, and you can have the weekend to yourselves."

They decided to go and see the family for the weekend to tell them the news. They went to Susie's mother and father first, and got drunk that night.

Trixy was happy to see her cousins – one in particular, her best friend, Muggy. She told her all about the boy at the farm, and they chatted like young girls do. Muggy said, "What if he asks you to marry him?"

"Don't be foolish, Muggy, I only met him the once. And he isn't a tinker, so I cannae."

"Well, you can dream and pretend, can't you?" Muggy replied.

They left there the next day and went to visit her father's parents, Jessie and Davie.

"Hello there Wuggie, what are you doing here the day?"

"Well, we have a bit of news for you. I am going to be a faither again."

"Oh, that's great. We will have to have a wee peeve[1] the night to celebrate."

So they all got drunk that night again, but an argument broke out between two silly laddies over some lassie from another camp. Well, all hell broke loose. Everybody was fighting – men,

1. drink

women and kids. The noise was terrible. One of the wee laddies went down for the police, and they came up, but no way would they interfere with a tinkers' fight, so they went away again.

The fight lasted well into the night. When they were tired they fell asleep where they lay.

The next morning, what a state the camp was in. Even Trixy's mother had a black eye. There were bleeding noses, black eyes galore, and men walking holding their sides. There were a few ribs broken as well.

Susie and Wuggie packed their things in the pram they had, called to the kids and away they went to go back to their camp.

Then Susie started on to Wuggie. "How come every time we go to your folk there is always a fight breaks oot?"

"Ah, they needed a wee fight to make the party complete."

"Well, if that's what you think, Wuggy, next time you can go yourself."

Trixy thought to herself, if the farmer was back home as he was supposed to be, then so was Bobby. On the Monday, she went up to the farm as usual for milk and tatties, and Bobby was there. She was so excited to see him she turned shy, and hung her head.

"Hi there," said Bobby in a cheery voice, "what have you been up to?"

Well, she told him all about the drinking and fighting, the black eyes and bloody noses.

"Well," said Bobby, "you ken how to make a man laugh, yes, you sure do. I thought that it was normal for tinkers to fight?"

"Indeed it is not. My mother's family never fight with a drink in them. You're no' being cheeky, are you? Throwing tink in my face isn't nice."

"Oh, I didn't mean any harm by it. I ken nothing aboot tinkers. You are the only one I have ever spoke to, and you are nice."

Trixy blushed at that remark. They then had a long chat about anything that came into their minds. Then Trixy headed home.

When she got there, her mother and her father were having an argument as usual about the fighting at the party. Trixy ignored them and went away to reminisce on her own, thinking about Bobby.

She saw a bush moving, and when she went to investigate what it was, there was Bobby staring at her.

"What are you doing there?" she asked.

"Hoping to see you," he said.

They went for a walk, and after that, this happened every night. They were drawn together like magnets. They fell in love.

Trixy knew full well her family would never allow her to marry Bobby. He wasn't one of her kind. So the couple kept their secret for months, until one day her mother said to her, "You are awful peaky-looking this morning, are you alright?"

"Yes," she replied, so fast that her mother was a bit suspicious.

Trixy had known for a few days she was with child, and Bobby was the father.

The tone of her mother's voice that day awakened something in her. She flew up to the farm in a panic to tell Bobby. He wasn't there. The farmer's wife said he had gone away that morning. To work on another farm, where his girlfriend was.

"Girlfriend?" said Trixy.

"Oh yes – they are to be married next month. Her father is a gentleman farmer. I thought he would have told you about her."

"No, he never told me."

"He left this note for you, and told me to give it to you when I saw you."

Trixy looked at the note, but she couldn't read and so she had no idea what it said. The farmer's wife knew this, so she said to her, "Give it back to me, lass, and I will read it to you."

She read it out. "'Dear Trixy, it was good while it lasted, but you know I could never marry a tinker girl. All the best, Bobby.' Oh my goodness, were you and he…!" The woman was stuck for words.

Trixy ran away from the woman as quickly as she could, like she had with her mother, before she could guess the truth about her condition. She ran and ran, away from the direction of the tent. She never came home all night or the next day. Her mother and father were going mad with worry.

Late the following afternoon a policeman arrived. He came out with it bluntly. "We have just pulled your Trixy out of the water – drowned, she is."

After the funeral they left that area, never to go back there ever again. Later on, Trixy's mother Susie had a wee girl who they called Bella, but they never got over the shock of losing Trixy.

Canty Auld Wife

This is a poem my mother received from an old woman. She was an old woman on her own and had no family. She died many, many years ago. It is more like a story in rhyme than a poem. She composed it herself, and gave it to my mother. It is a true, tragic story about things that happened in her life.

I'm a canty auld wife, near the close o' life's span,
And it's mony lang years since I lost my guid man,
And my three bonny laddies sae gallant and brave,
For they're a' sleepin soond, in yon far distant grave.

Fae bairnies tae manhood, I reared them wi' care,
But wi' the want o' their faither the struggle was sair,
And when war was declared, and we fought wi' the Huns,
Richt prood was I then o' my three gallant sons.

For proudly and blithely they answered the ca',
Brave, stalwart and kilted they a' gaed awa',
And though at the partin, my heart nearly brack,
But I hadnae the wish tae keep ane o' them back.

For I kent as I watched them as far's I could see,
That they would a' be heroes for Scotland and me,
So I slipped awa' intae my ain fireside,
And I prayed that the Lord in his mercy would guide,

And guard my dear laddies through war's deadly strife,
That he in his mercy would spare their young life.
Noo a letter fae Donald cam hame the next week,
And I smiled wi' the tears rinnin doon o'er ma cheek.

"Aye keep up your heart, mither, we will soon see it
    through,
For ye ken every Jock has a mither like you,
Wha expects that their sons will dae mair than his part,
We will soon be hame, mither, aye keep up yer heart."

Noo I tried tae be cheery, though oft I was wae,
Till the time slipped by till a cauld snawy day,
And my mind wi' an evil forbodin was filled,
For the post brought me word that my Donald was killed.

Noo, Donald was the youngest, and sair was the blow,
Till my fu' cup o' sorrow had to overflow,
For Sandy was slain ere the auld year had set,
And Geordie was missin, he is aye missin yet.

Sair, sair, was my heart, but the time slippet past,
Till warfare was ended, and peace came at last,
And mothers o' heroes maun just be as brave,
So I dried up my tears, and rejoiced wi' the lave.

Ah, but noo as I sit wi' a tear in my e'e,
And think o' my laddies I nae mair can see,
Wha, for king and for country, gi'ed up their young lives,
But I am prood o' my heroes, a Scottish auld wife.

Hairy Susan

There was an old woman away up past Pitlochry, and every day she put a pot of soup on for the travellers that came to her door selling their wares, or just coming for a bowl of her soup. She had a garden full of fresh vegetables, her soup was out of this world, and the civility she showed to the travellers was great. She treated them as she treated anyone, with kindness and concern. Often she would let them sleep in her shed for the night, when they were passing through.

There was one thing about this old woman, she had a full grown beard, just like a man's. It was all over her face and hung down about six inches past her chin. To the travellers that knew her it didn't matter, and if they told other travellers about her soup, they would warn them about her beard, so they knew what to expect. Her name was Susan Moir, but travellers always had other names for folk, and they called her Hairy Susan. She didn't know they called her that, because they called her Susan to her face.

One day an old man came to Susan's door and rapped. His name was Shitey Tam. Well, that's what the travellers called him. He would be about fifty years of age, and the reason they called him Shitey Tam was he never cleaned his arse when he geared,[1] and there was always a smell and a hum off him. He had a wee dog called Mick. It was a brown brindled dog, a quiet wee crater.

Now Tam could only see out of one eye, and even that was a wee bit blurry. When Susan answered the door, she told him to come awa in, and get some soup. He never noticed the beard

1. shit

on her, and he sat down on her couch, thanking her all the time for being so kind to him.

"Where are you headed, laddie?" she asked him.

"Well, I was thinking aboot going to Alyth to pick the berries."

"I could give you a few days' work," she said. "My garden needs weeding, and my berries need to be picked, and my strawberries as well."

"That would be fine," he said to her. So she showed him the shed where he could kip down with his wee dog.

He got settled for the night, and he was thinking to himself, "This is a cushy place, plenty habbin,[1] and a job as well. I might stay on for a while," he thought. Then he fell asleep.

Next morning she woke him up with a cup of tea. "Here you are, you can get your breakfast when you come in to the hoose."

He drank his tea, and he was on top of the world with the service she was giving him. Tea in bed! He thought, "Cannae be bad, eh!" He thought to himself, "You have landed on your feet this time, Tam, my old boy."

He went into the house and had his breakfast. A bowl of brose, thick with pepper just the way he liked it.

He stayed a while with the old woman, and one day she said to him, "Tam, I like your company. Are you married?"

"Oh, dear me, no, woman, I never was. Women wasn't my strong point, but I have had my moments, I must say."

"Good," she said. "Now listen, Tam, I have a proposal for you."

"I'm no' marrying you."

"No, no, don't be silly," she said. "We are too auld for that. But will you move in with me, to the house, and keep me warm in the winter time? We get on so well, and I am gey lonely, and I would miss you now if you went away."

"Well, let me think about it, and I will let you know in the morning."

1. food

So off he goes to his bed, and he couldn't sleep for thinking about what she had said to him. He thought to himself, "I would be mad to give this all up, and wander about the country again. I'm no' getting any younger, and I need to settle down. I cannae see her right, but what does that matter? She is kind and cooks barry habbin.[1] I think I will stay. I'll tell her in the morning." Then he fell asleep, thinking to himself, "She is handing it to me on a plate. What man would turn that doon?"

Next morning he told her of the decision he had made, and she was over the moon. "Well, you might as well move in tonight."

"I will," he said, and went to do his work. That night, after they had their supper, she said to him, "Are you ready for bed then, Tam?"

"Aye, I am that."

So they got into bed, and put the light out. He slipped his hand over to her. Then he shouted, "Oh my God, oh my God, you're a man!"

"Aye, did you no ken that?"

"No, I didn't!"

He jumped out of the bed, opened the door, and never stopped till he landed in Alyth. That is where he told us this story.

We didn't know whether to believe him or not, but the travellers still carried on going to Hairy Susan's for their soup.

1. good food

True Love

The minute Eddie saw Maureen, he fell in love with her. She had blond hair, green eyes, and her hair was down to her waist. They were camped at Fortingall, and the first time he saw her, she was with her father putting down lime-sticks to catch birds. They weren't after ordinary birds, but rare ones. This was another job travellers did to make money, and they sold the birds to pet shops.

When Eddie got back to his family, he discovered that Maureen had a man already. He was called Ike. Eddie went into his tent grief-stricken, but what could he do? Nothing!

There were four tents at this camp, and they were there for the winter months. That was the best time to catch the birds, because they were hungry and came down for the bread that was left beside the lime-twigs. The twigs were made so that they were sticky and the birds stuck to them. It didn't hurt the birds at all.

Eddie didn't do lime-sticks: he sold baskets and wooden flowers. He made the flowers out of what travellers called the bull tree – I don't know the proper name of the wood. It was soft in the centre.

He was in his tent one day when his mother came in, and said a man wanted to speak to him. When he came out of the tent, Maureen was there with the young man. Eddie knew right away that this was Ike, her boyfriend. "Do you make wooden flowers?" Ike asked.

"Yes, I do," said Eddie.

"Well, me and my girl here would like to buy some. We have a funeral to go to in two days time, and need flowers for it. How much are they?"

"Sixpence each with the privet." (Privet was what they called greenery they picked off the hedges, it made the flowers look nice.)

"That's fine," said Ike, "we will take a dozen. Can we pick them up tomorrow, then?"

"Aye, they will be ready for you then."

When dinnertime came, Eddie said to his Da, "That man o' Maureen's speaks awfy funny."

"Did you no ken? He's English. He comes from away down south somewhere, Cambridge or something like that."

"How did Maureen meet him, then?"

"They went down south to pick fruit, and she met him there. How, laddie, you dinnae fancy her, do you?"

"No, Da, dinnae be thickent.[1] I was just wondering. They have ordered a dozen flooers aff me, and I have to have them ready the morn."

"That's fine," said his Da, "well done."

The next day Maureen came herself to collect the flowers.

"They are all ready and done."

"Thanks," said Maureen, "they look great. It's a cousin of mine that has died, and she's getting buried in Dunkeld."

"Oh, I am sorry," said Eddie.

"Don't be. She was the most aggravating woman God put on this earth. She stole my first boyfriend. She ran away with him, but he beat her to death. Serves her right, but I suppose she saved me from being the one who got hit. The funeral is at twelve tomorrow. See you later," and she skipped away.

Eddie's heart was pounding like a hammer with the very thought of her. He was angry with himself for feeling like this. It was a new feeling for him, and although it was exciting, it was hurting as well.

He got stuck into some work making baskets, as his stock was getting low, and so were his flowers. He worked all day. He made three tirly[2] baskets and a few flowers as well. His heart wasn't in it, but his family needed the money.

1. stupid   2. round

Next day, about four o'clock, he heard a noise on the lane, and when he looked out it was Maureen's man, Ike, and another man fighting. Maureen was trying to get her man away, but he was well drunk, and paid no attention to her at all.

It was a real fight, not just a skirmish. They were knocking lumps out of each other. There was blood everywhere. The other man was saying to Ike, "You started all this fighting and arguing. Why?"

"You insulted my friend that came up for the funeral!"

"No, no," said the man. "He called me a Scotch bastard, then you came here, followed me up the lane and started fighting with me."

"He said you were calling him names."

"That's why I fought with you. So we will just carry on till someone gets knocked out." Wallop, wallop, on they fought. Ike was really knocking hell out of this man.

Eddie's dad and his brother stopped it. The Scots man was lying in a pool of blood, and they held onto Ike. More travellers came to the scene and took the unconscious man into one of their tents.

Ike was still struggling and shouting, "I've won, I've won!"

"What do you mean," asked Eddie's father.

"Well," said Ike, "I am a boxer, a bare-knuckle fighter, and that's what I do in England. I travel all over, fighting the hard men among the travellers' camps, and they put bets on me, and I can win a lot of money. So I am trying to break into Scotland, and make more money."

Maureen, when she heard that, was so disgusted with him, she shouted, "You never cared for me, it was only so you could get into Scotland!"

"Yes, you are right. I have a woman in England and three kids, and I leave here tomorrow to go back to my family."

"You are going right now," said Maureen, "and never show your face here again."

Ike got his things from the tent, and was escorted down the lane, and Eddie shouted good riddance. Everything calmed down for the rest of that day, and everyone was glad.

The next day Eddie went down by the river to get some more wands to make his baskets, and he found Maureen sitting by the river, playing with a stick, and she looked very sad. Eddie went up to her and said, "I am so sorry for what happened yesterday. You must be hert sick with losin yer man."

"Me sick with losing that no good man! No, I am relieved."

"Well, there is something bothering you, Maureen, I can tell."

"Promise you won't say a word, then, Eddie, and I will tell you. I have to tell someone, or I am going to go moich.[1]"

"I would never tell anybody anything you tell me. You can trust me, honest to God."

"Well..." said Maureen. It seemed to stick in her throat, and she couldn't get it out. "I am... I am... going to have a bairn."

She spoke so fast and quick, he caught what she said and no more. He stared at her, not knowing what to say. He was dumbfounded. "A bairn?"

"Aye, a bairn. What am I going to dae? My father will kill me."

"No, he won't. You stayed with him as your man for a few months, and things happen."

"I never looked on it that way. You are right. He will be too glad to see the back of that Englishman."

It was a few days later that Maureen told her mother and father. They were fine with it, but they didn't want anyone to inform the father that Maureen was bygant.[2]

Maureen followed Eddie down to the burn when he next went to get the wands he had been steeping for his baskets.

"Eddie, you were right," she said. "My mother and father took it well enough, but the father of the child has never to find out about it."

"That's great, Maureen, but I am busy just now, and can't talk. I will see you later."

Maureen felt he was trying to get rid of her, and walked away very sad. What had she done to make him act like this to her?

1. mad   2. with child

Little did she know Eddie was dying inside with love for her, and thought he had to back off a bit. Never in a million years would she think of him in that way, a poor basketmaker with just £200 in savings.

So he stayed out of her way for a few days, till at last she walked up to him one day and said, "Eddie, what have I done for you to shun me the way your doing?"

"Nothing, lass, nothing at all. I wanted to leave you alone to get used to your new life, and didn't want to pester you."

"Can we become friends again? I miss your company," asked Maureen.

"Well, maybe. Let me think about it, and I will give you an answer tomorrow down at the river at two o'clock."

Maureen wondered, "Why does he have to think about it? It's either yes or no." She walked away not too happy at all.

Eddie never slept all that night. He was trying to sort things out in his mind.

At two o'clock the next day, they met by the river. Maureen sat down beside Eddie, and looked at him warily. "Well," she said, "What is it, pals or no pals?"

"Sorry, Maureen, it is no pals."

She stared at him, not believing what he had just said, and she started to cry. "Why?" she asked.

He reached for her hand. "Because I love you, Maureen, and pals wouldn't be enough for me."

She smiled and pressed his hand to her breast. "It's not enough for me, either."

He slowly took her in his arms and began to kiss her. They clung together in a long, long, kiss that they never wanted to stop.

"Oh, Eddie, I have never been kissed like that before."

"The reason for that was, the person that kissed you before never loved you as much as I do. I worship the ground you walk on, and have from the first moment I saw you."

They kissed again. Then Eddie said to her, "I want to take you as my wife."

"But Eddie, I carry another man's child – you can't want me in my condition."

"I would want you in any condition."

"We will tell our families in the morning."

They sat and held each other for a long time, kissing now and then. At last Eddie looked at her. "There is one thing, Maureen, I want to say, and you must agree. I won't put a finger on you for sex till the baby is born. I will love it as if it is my own, because I love bairns, but we won't seal our love together till the baby arrives. Do you agree?"

"I agree with all you have to say, Eddie."

They left the riverbank, and went home separately.

The next morning Eddie got his father and mother together, and they sat down in the tent. He said he wanted to speak to them urgently.

"Now listen, father, before you get angry wi' me. I have something to tell you and Ma. I am taking Maureen as a wife, and I will be bringing up her child as my own." Then he fell silent.

So did his mother and father, they just stared at him in disbelief. "You cannae mean that, Eddie," said his father, at last. "You would be taking another man's leavings."

"I wouldn't be the first, and I'll no' be the last, that did that, Da. I love her deeply, and she me, and we want to be together."

"You had better tell her folk what your intentions are, and see what they have to say about this moichness.[1]"

Eddie went and got Maureen, and they went to see her father and mother, and they told them what they wanted to do.

"You cannae bring up another man's bairn, Eddie. It's just no' done."

"We are in love, and with or without your blessing we are going to be together."

Maureen eventually had a wee girl. They lived happily together, and a year later they had a wee boy. He was called Eddie after his dad.

1. stupidity

The Virgin Piper

There was an old piper, and the only way he knew how to make money was to play his pipes. He played the streets, at games and any place there was a crowd of folk. He made enough money to keep the wolf from the door, but that was all.

He never got married, although he fancied a few women in his time, because he never had the courage to ask them even to go for a walk with him. So he never knew what being with a woman really meant – he had heard about love, but had no idea sex came into it at all. His father in his early days never told him about the birds and the bees. He thought he would find out for himself when he met a girl, but of course he never went out with any girl. He was now reaching the age of fifty-six and didn't know the facts of life.

He was a man who would never stay beside any other travellers. He always lived by himself. One day he was piping up at Oban, and he met a cousin of his that he hadn't seen for a long time. "Well, well," said his cousin, "Willie boy, I haven't seen you in an age. Where have you been hiding yourself?"

"Oh, you ken me, I like to be by myself, Dokie."

"Well, we are just camped no far fae here, come for a drap tea, and we will hae a wee crack."

So Willie put his pipes in their box and followed Dokie home to the camp. When they got there, there were two woman making tea. Willie started to act shy now he had seen the morts.[1] Dokie knew this would happen, and said to Willie, "Come and sit beside the fire, Willie boy, and meet my wife and her sister May. You didnae ken I had a mort to myself, did you?"

"No," said Willie "I didnae ken at a'."

1. women

98

He was handed a big mug of tea and a lump of bread. He just realised he was very hungry, and ate it up as if he hadn't seen food for a month, smacking his lips as he ate.

"My, my, Willie boy, you are certainly enjoying that bit of duchil.[1]"

"Aye, I was a bit hungry."

Dokie's wife was named Chooks, a pet name Dokie had for her. What her real name was, Willie didn't know. Then he introduced Willie to May, a plump lassie, not very bonny and not very shy either. She was about thirty-five or thereabouts. She kept looking at Willie. Although he was quite old, he looked fit enough, and that took her fancy.

"Well," said Dokie, "What aboot me and you playing the street the morn thegither, for old times sake? We haven't done that for a few years, eh, Willie boy?"

"Oh well, alright, that will be fine wi' me. Halves as usual?"

"Yes, that's fine," said Dokie. Then Willie went away home to his own tent.

He turned and tossed all night. He couldn't get May out of his mind. Lying in his bed, he thought to himself, "Has she cast a spell on me? No, I never even spoke to her."

Why couldn't he get her out of his head? He knew women were only good for washing, and cleaning, making the food, and for company. Why was he smitten with her? He thought he was going moich.[2] At last he fell asleep, mumbling her name.

Next morning he actually washed his face, a thing he never usually did for weeks on end. His face was cleaner, but the dirt was so ingrained, it would take more than a few washes to clean it, even with soap, a thing he had never possessed.

He met Dokie in the town, and they started to play the street with their pipes. Willie laid down his pipes and started to dance the highland fling. He was a great dancer, but he hadn't done it for a very long time, because he was always alone, and no one was usually there to play the pipes for him. He got tired very easily.

1. bread   2. mad

"I am getting too auld for dancing now," he said.

"Not at all," said Dokie. "You were great, man."

They made a good lot of money between them, and went back to Dokie's camp to share it. They had ten shillings each, and in those days, to them, that was a fortune.

When they got back to the camp Chooks had a pot of soup ready for them, and they ate their fill. "My God," said Willie, "that was a braw bowl of soup. It was very tasty, Chooks."

"Oh, I didn't make it, May did."

His eyes caught May's, and she looked down with a twitch of a smile on her lips. He could only stare at her without saying anything at all. He was speechless.

"Tomorrow again, Willie boy?" asked Dokie.

"Aye, that will do me fine."

"We will have a good drink this weekend out of this, eh, Willie?"

"I'm all for that," said Willie.

When Saturday came, they bought a carry-out, some whisky, and settled down to a drinking session. The woman joined in too. They were sitting round the fire slugging down the whisky as if it was going out of fashion. They were getting merrier and merrier, and were singing the old-fashioned songs. They had a great time.

Dokie asked Willie if he was going for a sloosh,[1] because he had something to say to him. So off the men went into the bushes. "Now," said Dokie, after he had a sloosh, "what do you think of May?"

"What do you mean, what do I think o' May?"

"Willie boy, she would make a good wife tae you, and you would never be lonely again in your life."

"A wife – I'm no' seeking a wife. What would I do wi' her?"

"She will cook for you, clean for you and make food for you, and keep you warm in the winter," he said, with a twinkle in his eye. Little did he know that Willie knew nothing about sex, and never imagined it was a part of marriage.

1. pee

"Well, I am no' going to marry her, ye ken. She can be my wife, and that's it, nae marriage ceremony."

"I will tell you what I will do," said Dokie. "I will marry you two, and that can be an excuse for a peeve.[1]"

"Yes, that will do," said Willie boy, "I will agree to that."

"Well, you had better go and ask her to marry you, then."

"No' me. Can you ask her for me, please, Dokie?"

So Dokie went and asked May if she would marry Willie boy. Her face lit up like a beacon, and she agreed.

So next day was to be the wedding, such as it was. May got a loan of a frock from Chooks, which was far too small for her. She had no decent shoes, so she put on her boots with the toes peeping out, and she was as happy as Larry. She was the happiest bride in Scotland that day.

"Wait a minute," said Chooks, "you cannae get married without combing your hair."

"But I haven't got a comb," said May.

"Wait there," said Chooks, "I will be back in a minute."

Away she went and got a big limb of broom, and came back with it, and she raked it over May's hair. "There, that will do now, you're bonny enough."

The four of them gathered round the fire. Dokie didn't know what to say, so he made it up as he went along. "You are now man and wife, God bless the both of you." He was dying to get into the drink, so he hurried it up.

"How do you feel, Willie boy, now that you are married?"

"I don't feel any different, am I supposed to?"

"Yes, you are supposed to, and you have to kiss the bride."

"I never kissed a woman in my life, no' even my mother."

"You have to now, to seal things final."

So he kissed May on the cheek, then spat onto his dirty sleeve and rubbed his tongue with it. They got down to some serious drinking. It had been a good day, but they all fell asleep round the fire, and that was them till morning.

They awoke up one at a time, in the doldrums of drink,

1. drink

101

and their tongues stuck to the tops of their mouths. They were parched for a drink of water. Willie and Dokie staggered down to the wee burn, and lay down on the bank with their tongues in the water.

"Leave some for me," shouted May, and she also drank out of the burn.

May put the kettle on to make a drop of tea for her new husband, and was humming as she did so. When the men came back to the camp, Willie boy said to the others, "Come and get a cup of tea at my tent." He was frightened to be alone with May, because he did not know what to say to her.

"Na, na," said Dokie. "You go away to your tent and get your tea. Chooks will be waiting for me."

So, slowly Willie made for his tent, where the tea was waiting for him, and May had made toast for him as well. "This is great," he thought, "it's no' bad having a wife after a'."

He sat down and had his breakfast beside his wife, and they chatted away about the marriage the day before, and the good drink they had had. Willie boy seemed more relaxed in May's company now, but he thought to himself, it is early days yet.

May tidied up and did some washing and put the dinner on for that night. Rabbit they were having, and tatties.

At night after they got their food, May started to yawn. "Oh, I am dead tired. I think I'll awa' to bed."

Willie looked at her. "Where are you going to sleep, May?"

"Wi' you in your bed, of course, all wives sleep with their man."

"Ah well," thought Willie, "I suppose that's what I have to dae, if that's what all men dae."

May crawled into bed and took her clothes off, and snuggled down, waiting for Willie to come to bed. She was in anticipation of her first night with her new husband. Her new, strong husband, she thought.

Willie doused out the fire, and came to bed. He crawled in with all his clothes on, and settled down. "You cannae come to bed with all your clothes on," said May.

"I have never slept wi' my clothes aff in all my life, woman, and I am no' starting now."

"Your clothes are rubbing against my body, and it will get scourged."

"Well, well, I will take my jacket off, will that please you?"

"What aboot your troosers as well?"

"Well, if it keeps you quiet and makes you sleep, I suppose I'll take them off."

Half an hour later, Willie was snoring away. May thought it funny he didn't try something on her. So she put her hand over and started to play with him. He woke up, and gave a terrible roar out of him. "What are you doing, woman?"

"I am playing wi' your winkle."

"What?" he shouted, and he stirred and sat up and faced her. He lifted the covers and pointed down below. "That is private property, and you have no right touching it."

He felt a twitch, and he started to groan "Oh my God, woman, what have you done, it's swelling up now! You have given me a disease. What kind o' woman are you? A diseased wife I have got!"

He jumped out of the tent and sat down in a bucket of cold water, and his winkle went back to normal.

"Don't you ever come near me again, May," he shouted. "I am leaving you tomorrow, and you won't see me again!"

And that is what he did.

Nature and Sex

This story came from an old woman in the Borders, and it happened around the year of 1902. She told me the girl was a relation to her.

Maisie was a young girl about sixteen. She was full of life, and she had a boyfriend named Tookie. That wasn't his real name, but a name the travellers gave him. He was a bit of a harum-scarum lad, and was always getting into trouble with one traveller or another. He was food-mad, and if any traveller turned his back when they were eating round the fire, Tookie was away with the food. Maisie and Tookie were only good friends, but their parents thought some day they would get together.

One fine day, as they were walking through the wood near their camp, they came across a bird's nest that had fallen from a tree. There was one wee yunk[1] in it.

"Ah," said Maisie, "look at this, Tookie. Poor wee thing. Give me your bonnet to make a bed for it."

"I am no' giving you my bonnet for that ugly wee thing to gear[2] in it."

"Come on, noo, Tookie, look at its wee face."

So he handed her the bonnet. They sat down on the grass listening to the wee bird cheeping. Tookie said to her, "Where does wee birds come fae, Maisie?"

"From an egg, you fool, where else?"

"Aye, I ken, but who puts them in the egg?"

"The bird, of course."

"Aye," said Tookie. "But where does she get them fae?"

Maisie was stumped with that one. "Ask your faither when you go hame," said Maisie, "I don't know."

1. baby bird   2. shit

104

That night, after they had their habbin[1] Tookie said to his father, "Can I speak to you on your own, Faither?"

"What for, son?"

"It's private, Faither."

So they walked away from the others at the fire. "Faither, where does wee birds come fae?"

"The egg, thickent[2] laddie."

"Aye, but who puts it there?" Tookie asked.

"The mammy bird."

"But how? Where does she get it to put in the egg?"

The father shuffled about on his feet. "Well, that's a thing travellers never tell their sons and daughters. You learn that for yourself, as time goes on."

"Och, I'll ask my mither."

"Don't you dare. Do you hear me?"

"OK, OK, I won't. Dinnae shout at me, then."

A while later, he and Maisie had a walk down by the riverside.

"Well," said Maisie, "did you ask your faither, Tookie?"

"I did, Maisie, and he wouldn't tell me. He says I have to find it oot for myself, but how?"

Maisie lay down among the ferns, near the bank of the river, and Tooky spread out beside her. He was keeking[3] at her, and giving her funny looks.

"What's wrong wi' you, man, how are you looking at me like that?"

"I don't know, but you look different to me the night."

"What do you mean?"

"I feel things stirring in me, and I feel funny, Maisie, honest I do!"

"Och, awa' ye go, you thickent galoot, and behave yourself."

"Just let me kiss you, just once, Maisie."

"What, you fool? Why?"

"I don't ken, I just got an urge to kiss you."

"Well, awa' and kiss your auld dug. You fool o' a laddie that you are!"

1. food   2. stupid   3. glancing over

105

"I also want to feel your pappies.[1]"

Maisie lifted her hand, and gave him such a wallop, he saw stars. "You dirty animal that you are!"

"Look, Maisie, I have figured it out myself. Looking at you we can make wee yunks wirself.[2]"

"How?" asked Maisie.

"Well, kiss me and we will find out. That's how we will discover where wee birds come fae."

"Alright, but if I dinnae get a yunk, you have had it."

He took her in his arms and kissed her. He started fumbling with her, and lifted her skirt and had his way with her, right there and then. They lay back pechin.[3]

"Will I get yunks noo?" asked Maisie.

"Maybe, aye. I hope so," said Tookie. "Don't tell anyone, mind, Maisie."

"I'm no thick like you, of course I won't tell."

They went back to the camp after that, and said nothing, but Maisie felt a bit guilty. Why, she didn't know. They were only going to have wee chicks, and that's not a bad thing, is it?

Tookie that night couldn't help thinking about Maisie, and what they had done. Was it wrong? How could it be wrong, when it felt so good? He finally fell asleep, thinking about it.

The next morning, Tookie's father announced they were moving. "But I cannae go now," he said to himself. "Maisie is having wee yunks."

"Come on noo, laddie, get packed up. We are shifting the day tae Ballater."

Tookie couldn't say anything to him, or he would find out what he had been up to. So he went to Maisie and told her he was moving. "If you have wee birds, will you keep me one, and I will get it later?"

"I will," said Maisie, saying goodbye to him.

Months passed, and of course Maisie had no wee birds. She was disappointed, and confessed to her mother everything, asking her why she had never had yunks.

1. breasts   2. ourselves   3. panting

"You silly, silly, lassie, wait till your faither comes hame and hears what you have been up to, he won't be pleased at all."

Maisie started to shake, now. "Did I do wrong, Mammy?"

"Aye, faith, you did wrong, alright. That's the way you get wains.[1] Maybe you're expecting."

"Expecting what, Mam?"

"A wain, you fool o' a lassie. That's how wains are made! You must wait till you have a man for that."

She wasn't with child, and she never had any yunks either.

The old woman told me at the end of the story it was herself that it had happened to. It was her own story she had told me. She finally married Tookie the next year, and they never forgot their stupidness of the year before. They had six bairns, and lived happy ever after – sometimes.

1. kids

The Donkey

A story I have come across a few times while I was out collecting stories from travellers, is the one about a donkey. It was told to me in two different versions, but the gist of the story is the same.

This story is about an Irish traveller family that came over to live in Scotland. Their name was Malvern. The man was called Francis and his wife Bridget. They had three sons and two daughters. The youngest son, Danny, was a weakly wee thing and always ailing. They were a close family, and very religious. Danny was aged ten, but looked much younger. They were having a bad time of it in Ireland with discrimination, and were practically run out of the country. This wasn't because they were bad, but because they were too soft, and the other travellers didn't like that.

They landed in Stranraer on the twelfth day of June, 1912. They lived in gellies,[1] and were coming to Scotland to stay and hawk for a living. They made their way up country, hawking all the way until they landed in a small town in Perthshire called Kinross.

Travellers in these days could camp anywhere freely. The Malverns were very content now that they were in Scotland.

One day Danny took ill with vomiting and was very poorly. His mother took him in a pram, and went down town to see a doctor. On the way she passed a cottage hospital, and decided to go in – there must be a doctor there, she thought. She slowly pushed the door open, and went in with the pram.

"You there, you can't come into hospital with a pram, it's not allowed." It was a very snooty nurse.

1. bow tents

"I am very sorry, ma'am, but my son can't walk, he is too ill. Is there a doctor around?"

Just at that moment a man came round the corner with a bunch of papers in his hand. "What's going on here?"

"Oh, Doctor Ramsay, the wee boy is sick and his mother wanted to see a doctor."

Looking down at Danny, the doctor could see he was very ill. "Very well, pick him up and come into my consulting room."

Bridget picked her wee boy up and took him into the surgery. The doctor gave him a thorough examination, and told him to lie on the bed while he had a word with his mother.

Outside the surgery the doctor took her to a waiting room, and bade her sit down. "Your little boy is very sick indeed. I would like to let a specialist see him, and I am afraid we will have to keep him in for a few days."

Bridget's face fell, and the doctor saw the worry come into her eyes. "You did the right thing to bring him here. We will look after him well, have no fear. You can come back tomorrow, and I might have more news for you about his condition. I will get the specialist here first thing in the morning."

When Bridget got home and told the boy's father, he went into a panic. "My child, my child! Is there is nothing we can do tonight?"

Said Bridget, "We will know better in the morning."

Next morning they went to the hospital about ten a.m. They walked up to the desk to speak to the nurse that was there. Bridget said "We have come to see our boy that was left here last night. His name is Danny Malvern."

The nurse opened the book of admissions and looked for the name. "Will you please have a seat in the waiting room," she said, "and I will tell the doctor you are here." They went into the room and waited there for half an hour. They were getting impatient at the delay. Then two doctors came in, the one from the night before, and a taller distinguished-looking one, and asked them to come to the consultant's room.

Francis and Bridget followed them into the room, and they were asked to sit down. There was concern on the faces of the two doctors. Bridget swallowed hard, making a noise.

"Now," said the consultant, "you both know that Danny is a very, very sick little boy."

They nodded in reply. "Well, I am afraid to have to tell you both this, but he has a blood disease, and I am afraid there is nothing we can do for him."

"What do you mean?" said Francis. "You are doctors, and you have the power to heal. Why can't you help our boy?"

"He is too far gone. Maybe two years ago he could have been saved, but now it is too late. The white cells in his blood are eating up the red cells, and there is no cure for this condition. Some days he will be better than others, but he will never get better from this illness. We are so sorry."

The mother and father bowed their heads in sorrow, hugging each other. The doctors said, "We will leave you a minute to compose yourselves," and left the room.

"Bridget, what are we going to do? Our poor wee boy," said Francis, then he burst out crying. This was a thing he never did in his life before, but he just let it all out, as they were sitting there in the waiting room hugging each other.

About ten minutes later the doctor came back. They were as composed as they could be. "Have you any questions you want to ask me?" the doctor said.

"Yes," said Bridget, "we have. What happens now?"

"Well, in a couple of days," said the doctor "you can take him home, when he regains his strength a bit, but remember we are always here if you need us."

"How long does he have?" asked a very sad Francis, not wanting to put that question, but knowing he had to.

"Six months at the most."

Trembling uncontrollably, Bridget stood up, wringing her hands in sorrow, and paced up and down the room.

"You can go and see him now," said the doctor.

"Wipe your tears, woman. We must go in and see him, and

no' let him know we are upset in any way," said Frances. They went into the ward to see Danny, and he looked a bit better, but weak, and he was propped up in the bed. They chatted to him for about half an hour until they saw he was getting tired, then they kissed him and went home to the camp.

Telling the other kids was very hard, and they all broke down and cried.

"We must hide it from him when he comes out of hospital in a few days time," said their father, "and do everything to please him, because we won't have him for long." His voice was cracking and trailing away with grief.

Two days later, Danny was allowed home. He walked out of hospital holding his mother's hand and smiling from ear to ear, happy that finally he was going home to his family. "The hospital is alright, Mam, but the bed, I couldn't sleep right in it, and the food wasn't that good either. Give me a camp any day."

Smiling, his mother hugged him tight to her breast, kissing him on the brow.

He got a good welcome when he got home from all the family and their wee dog Tizer.

Lying in bed that night, Francis said to his wife, "Now listen, anything Danny wants we must get him, to make him happy."

"Well, we can only try and do wir best," said Bridget.

A few days later Danny was sitting at the fire when his dad came back from the hawking. He jumped off the cart and walked over to where his son was sitting. "Hello there, my boy, how are you doing, and what are you up to?"

"Not much, Dad, just thinking to myself how I came to be ill, and I answered myself. It's God's will."

Not knowing what to say, his dad sat poking the fire thinking how to answer him. "Listen, Danny, me and your Ma last night were thinking, what would you like most in the whole wide world?"

Danny's eyes popped out of his head, and he stared with excitement. "Anything, dad?"

"Yes, of course, anything."

"I want a donkey, but it must be an Irish donkey."

His dad stared at him. "A donkey?"

"Yes, from Ireland. They are the real ones, aren't they, Dad?"

"Well, yes, I suppose they are, son."

"Will I get one?"

"Of course, my son, you can get one."

After dinner that night, the mother and father were talking at the fire, and the rest were in bed. "What we going to do, old wife, about this donkey?"

"We have to get it. You will have to go to Ireland and get one for him, and take Bernie with you to keep you company." Bernie was the second oldest son.

A week later, off they went to Ireland, Francis and Bernie. Danny was so excited he could hardly contain himself. "Hurry back, Dad. I'll be waiting for you."

"I will that, son. Be good, and look after yer Ma while I am away." They hugged him and went away.

§

It was early morning when they arrived in Ireland, and Francis knew where to look for a donkey. There was a man called Seth Riley who always had donkeys. So they made their way to where he was camped. It wasn't too far from the boat at Larne. It took them a few hours to walk there, but they arrived at the camp at eleven a.m.

Seth was just getting up, and had the kettle on. "Hello there, Francis. It's a long time since I saw you. Come in about and tell us what you are up to these days."

Francis told him why they were in Ireland: to buy a donkey for Danny.

"Well, I have three donkeys. A two-year-old, a five-year-old and a ten-year-old." They sounded good to Frances. "What's the price of them?"

"The two-year-old is ten pounds. The other two are five pounds each. They are a bargain, Francis, you know that."

Francis was thinking it over, and wandered away by himself to consider his choice. He decided he would take the five-year-old, for five pounds, and he came back and told Seth this.

"We will leave in the morning, and get back to Scotland with the donkey."

They slept underneath a bush that night, and were up very early next morning to get the boat back to Scotland. It took them all that day and all the next day to get back to where they were staying. They arrived at midday and were weary and exhausted.

No one was there at the camp. Bridget was at the shops and the rest would be out hawking. Francis took the donkey to the back of the bushes where the tent was. It was eating the succulent grass growing there, and he left a bucket of water for it, so it was very content. He and Bernie made something to eat, had two big jugs of tea and fell asleep at the fire.

An hour later all the rest of the family came home, and were so pleased that Francis and Bernie were back again. Danny gave a loud scream when he saw his dad.

"Come with me, little man," Francis said, and taking him by the hand he led him to the donkey.

There was never a happier boy in all the land that day. "Mam, can I sleep with the donkey tonight?"

"No, son, you can never sleep with the donkey, because you know you are not well. But you will have him all day."

His father then said to him, "You can't keep calling him donkey, you must give him a name, Danny, a name you like."

"Oh yes," said Danny, "I must." He turned around and went to where the donkey was tethered. He looked hard and long into the donkey's face, wondering, "What is going to be your name?" He thought of a few names, but none of them fitted the look on the donkey's face. Then it came to him, a name just popped into his head. Joseph!

He ran to his mother and father, so excited. "I have a name for my donkey, Dad!"

"What is it, son?"

"Joseph, but Joe for short." The family looked at one another and smiled, and that smile was one of approval.

Danny didn't die in six months, as the doctors had said he would. He lived for another ten years after that, and they all thought it was due to the same thing. It was because of Joseph the donkey, and the power of God.

Redhead

This is a story I got away up in the north of Scotland, in Aberdeenshire.

There was a travelling family who stayed five miles north of Aberdeen. They were a father and mother, two girls and one boy.

This story is about the boy, who was named Doddie after his father. All he ever thought about for years was going off to sea with a fishing boat. He was adamant he was going to be a fisherman, no matter what, but there was one problem – a big problem. He had red hair, and he knew that would stop him from ever getting on a fishing boat. It could never be. Fishermen just wouldn't let a red-haired person on their boat. If they saw a person with red hair when they were going to fish on any day, they would turn back and not go out that day.

This was heartbreaking for Doddie, and he fell into a deep depression. His mother and father tried everything to help him, but nothing worked. The sea seemed to be calling on him. He would go out hawking with his father every day, but when he came home he would mope round the fire at night.

One evening his father said to him, "Doddie, come on, let's play a game of quoits." So he got up from the fire and played quoits with his father.

An hour later there was a sound of someone coming, and they looked up. It was Beer-belly Willie – that's what the travellers called him anyway, his real name was Willie Shanks.

He wasn't a traveller, but lived like one, he and his wife Susie and their lassie. They called her Lollipop. She was sixteen years old, but her face, God forgive me, looked like an old woman's.

115

She wasn't wrinkly, but old-looking. She had the knowledge of a grown woman, and she could sing like a linty.[1]

Beer-belly Willie had a belly as big as a bass drum. He had never seen his feet for years, or anything else down there for that matter. He was a nice man, but he was in his own road, as travellers would say. His wife was a thin woman, and she walked with a limp. She wasn't always a very pleasant woman, sometimes being sarcastic to Willie and Lollipop. The travellers had given her a nickname too – they called her Fungus Face. She had layers of skin lying on top of one another on her face where skin shouldn't be.

They came over to Doddie, the father, and asked if it would be alright to camp beside them for a few days. "Yes, surely, we will be glad of the company." So they put up their tent, and went for some fresh straw from the farm to make their beds. They made their tea and all sat round the fire, cracking and exchanging gossip.

The next morning early, the others were awakened by shouting coming from Willie and Susan's tent. The two of them were arguing hell for leather. Willie was shouting, "You leathery-faced woman, awa' doon tae the cobblers and get me a pair of boots, there's as much leather on your face that would make two pairs!"

She started to scream back at him, "Well, if that's so, how did you come to take up wi' me, then?"

Willie said to her, "You dinnae look at the mantlepiece when you're poking the fire!"

"You big-bellied swine that you are! Go and put the kettle on, I am dying for a cup of tea." And that was the argument over – as quick as it started, it finished. Old Doddie thought to himself, "Aye, there are queer folk in the shows." This was a saying he had heard from his mother many a time, and she was right.

Young Doddie went about with Lollipop a lot. They went for walks in the wood, and became good friends. She taught

1. linnet

him a lot, and they spoke often about the sea, a subject Doddie never got tired of. One day, as they were walking through the woods, Lollipop said to Doddie, "I was trying to think, last night, of how you can go to sea if you want to, and I came up with something."

Doddie was very, very excited and overjoyed. "What is it?" he asked her. "Hurry up and tell me quick."

"Well," said Lollipop, "we can dye your hair a different colour."

"Oh my God," said Doddie, "I never thought of that! You are great, Lollipop. If I could do that, that would be my problem sorted."

Doddie told his mother and father what he was going to do. Their question was, "Dye it with what?" So he ran to Lollipop and asked her.

"Boot-polish, you fool, black boot-polish."

"Hip, hip hooray!" shouted young Doddie, and he and Lollipop went to the shop for black boot-polish. It was only a penny a tin, so he bought two tins to keep him going.

That night, Lollipop started to put the black polish on his head to get rid of his red hair. She combed it in, then brushed it in, and his hair went pure black. "Now," said Lollipop, "you will have to sit away from the fire till it dries proper."

So young Doddie climbed up a tree, where there was a breeze blowing, and settled himself there for an hour. Then he came down. "Oh my God," he said, "my hair is as stiff as a board, this will never dae!"

The rest of the folk at the camp were killing themselves laughing, so Doddie started to laugh as well. "Och, I can't be bothered with the sea any more. I would rather stay on land."

He had fallen in love with Lollipop. They stayed together till they died, but never had any family.

Wartime Stories

❧

Travellers and the Army

Here are a few of the things that travellers did to keep from going into the army, when conscription came in at the start of the Second World War.

We went to visit some travellers one day on a Sunday, which was our visiting day. When we arrived at the campsite we found there were a good few camps there along the old road. One of my father's cousins was there. So we sat down by a big fire and had some tea.

A few minutes later this girl came up to the tent, said nothing, and went into the tent. She was walking very awkwardly in high heels.

My father asked his cousin who she was. She said she was giving her shelter for a few days. He didn't give it another thought.

My father bought some tyres and some scrap from these travellers, and said he would be back next day to collect it. The next day I went along with my father to collect the tyres and the scrap. When we got there, there was no one around but this girl sitting at the big fire, drinking tea. She wouldn't speak to us, but signalled to us to sit down.

She had a lot of lipstick on her mouth, and a hat on her head, and those high heels on her feet. She stood up to go into the tent, then tripped and fell, just missing the fire. Her hat flew off, and a wig came off with it, and her frock went above her waist. We could see from that the "woman" was a man. It was my father's cousin's son.

"Well, God, I didn't want to bing[1] to the cleesties[2] but what buggered me was them silly high heels."

He was caught after a year, but was unfit for the army anyway. He failed his medical, after all that hiding in women's clothes.

§

There was another man who was called up. He was terrified at the thought he was to be in the army. So he started eating cotton wool, thinking that the sergeant would think it was foam coming out of his mouth.

That didn't work at all. So he started peeing the bed. Every night he did it, and he wouldn't take his bedclothes off, which meant he was soaking every morning. He didn't wash or shave either, and he was stinking.

He was sent for by the commanding officer to explain himself.

"I don't want to be in the army," he said.

"Well, you have got your wish," replied the officer. "You have a mastoid ear, and can't go. I just got the report this morning."

So he was the happiest man in Scotland that day. He thought about the torture he had gone through, when he hadn't needed to. The travellers got a good laugh at that one.

1. go   2. army

The Heroine

Travellers were also involved in the 1745 Rebellion, but are never mentioned, even though they played a big part in it. This is a story about a traveller family during this time.

There was a family called McPhee living in the time of the '45. They didn't want to be involved with all the carry-on, but they were dragged into it by other travellers.

Young Mary McPhee went for water one Sunday morning, and was filling her bucket at the stream. She was seventeen. She was a plain-looking girl with long, straight hair, but she had a great twinkle in her eye that could melt anyone's heart, and she was her father's favourite.

As she filled her bucket, she heard horses trotting down the lane. She left the bucket and hid behind a big boulder.

Two men stopped to water their horses and drink themselves, and she could hear them talking. They were two redcoats, and as they spoke English it was difficult for Mary to make out what they said, as her own tongue was Gaelic. However she knew other travelling folk who spoke Scots, and heard them say something about going to burn out some houses up the glen.

While she was hiding behind the stone a man-keeper walked over her bare feet. She took the shawl from her shoulders and packed it in her mouth to keep herself from screaming. Finally the men mounted their horses and galloped away towards the top of the glen.

Mary got the water and headed back to camp. There were a lot of travellers on this camp site, with many different names, but mostly they were McPhees. Mary ran to tell her father what

1. lizard

she had heard the two redcoats say. Her father called all the travellers together and told them the news, about the plan to burn the houses.

"We will have to do something," said big Angus McPhee. "We cannae let them perish wi' fire."

So they decided to send two brothers to tell the folk who lived in the village at the top of the glen what was going to happen. They were only away for an hour. One of the men came back wounded, his leg severely damaged, and he was carrying his dead brother on his back.

They buried the brother, and the next day the other one died. The whole camp was in mourning. "If only we had stayed out of it," said big Angus, "they twa laddies wid be alive today, how stupid I was."

"No," said Mary, "you weren't stupid, Daddy, you should have sent me to go and tell them."

"You?" said her father, "I couldn't send my wain on a message like that, look what happened to your cousins."

"Aye, but I ken the moors like no one else kens them, and I can go like a whitrick.[1] So give me your blessing, Daddy, because I am going, and you cannae stop me."

So away Mary went to the village, about four miles away from the travellers' encampment. Her dress was torn and frayed at the bottom, and she never wore shoes ever, but, my goodness, she could fly through the heather, and hide when she had to.

When she got to the village the folk wouldn't believe her at first, they thought a tinker couldn't possibly know anything about redcoats, but Mary could be very persuasive. Finally they headed for the hills, to a spot where they could watch the village below. Sure enough, twenty or so redcoats appeared with torches, set fire to their houses, then galloped away.

"Now, didn't I tell you?" said Mary.

"Aye, you did, lass, and saved all our lives."

"What are you going to do now?" asked Mary. "Your houses are destroyed."

1. stoat

"Oh, that's nothing, lass. The rest of our families will look after us alright. Thanks again, lass."

Mary said goodbye and wandered back to the camp.

Just as she came to the stream where she got the water, humming away to herself, someone came and pounced on her. It was a redcoat. Mary was terrified, but held her head up high. "What do you want, redcoat? You better no' touch me, because I am a tinker, and I can put a curse on you, ye ken."

He dragged her behind the big stone she had hidden behind the last time, and pressed her up against it. "I need a woman," said the redcoat, "I am desperate."

"There are plenty sheep on the hills that will see to your needs, but if you touch me, this night you will die."

He carried on pressing her up against the big stone, but then thought better of it, and ran away up the hill. "Poor wee sheep," thought Mary.

When she got back to the camp, her father ran to meet her. "Oh, my lassie, you're back safe!"

"Aye," said Mary, "it would take more than a redcoat to stop me." Of course she didn't tell her father what had happened on her way home.

Mary became a runner for the clans up in the Highlands. She was greatly respected by the folk there, and she saved many a life. Mary herself died at the age of thirty. She was raped to death by ten redcoats on the moors.

She was a heroine in her time. They say there is a pile of stones built in her honour. Yes, Mary McPhee was one of a kind. She never married, but lived doing the thing she loved, helping her fellow Scots.

I got this story from an old traveller man. His age was 72. Two days after he told me the story, he died.

A Second World War Story

Hendry was a traveller who had never been away any place in his life, and when the Second World War began, he told his mother and father he wanted to join the army. They weren't too pleased about it, but he was old enough to make up his own mind. So he went and joined up in Perth. He had training to do, and he was excited about that, because he had always kept himself fit.

He went to the training camp, and came out with flying colours. He got a wee bit bullied, but not too much, because there weren't many folk who would meddle with him.

He was sent to Fort George for a few months till his posting came through. He did very well up there as well. He noticed when he went up there that there were a lot of very young laddies had joined up, and he thought to himself, they don't know what they are going to have to face, they are only bairns.

There was this young lad, and they called him Wedgie. The soldiers gave nicknames to their fellow soldiers just the same as travellers did. Hendry got very fond of Wedgie, because he was a weepy boy, especially at night. You would hear him multing[1] in his bed, but in the morning he would be fine again.

One day the sergeant came into the barracks and told them the postings had come through, and they had to be on the parade ground, with full kit, in ten minutes, because the captain was going to announce them. They were all excited about it, and made a mad rush to get ready. They were all lined up on the parade ground when the captain arrived with the papers.

"Well, men," he said, "you are fully fledged soldiers now, and ready for war."

1. crying

He started calling out the names, and Hendry was to be sent to France. Wedgie was sent to some place in England. He wasn't very happy, because he wasn't going to be with Hendry, but as Hendry told him, they would meet some time again, maybe at the war in France.

"Well, good luck," he said to Wedgie the next day, as they all went their different ways. Hendry got on the army ship with all the other soldiers that were going to France. He was excited, but wary as well. He didn't know what he was going to have to face once he came off the boat at the other side.

They landed in France and disembarked from the boat, and were ordered to stand to attention. Then they were led away to the barracks, such as they were. They were the poorest barracks any of them had ever seen, just wooden huts with no beds in them. They were given a blanket each, and that was their bed.

They were called to the eating quarters by the corporal. When they arrived there they were handed a tin mug of tea with no sugar or milk, and a thick slice of bread, and that was their meal for the day. They were told to take it back to their barracks and eat it, then go to bed.

In the room there were about twenty soldiers. There were only two gas lights, and it was very dim in there. They ate their bread, but Hendry threw his tea out the door. He couldn't drink it without sugar and milk.

The next morning they were called out of bed at six o'clock, with a terrific shout from a sergeant. "Get up, men, you are leaving today for the front line, so be prepared!"

They jumped out of their blankets and got ready. Their breakfast was a bowl of very thin porridge, and again no milk. So they just drank it from the bowl.

They were taken to the front line to relieve the men who were there, and who had been there for months. When they arrived they found a sight worse than they could ever have imagined. The men were in trenches full of mud, they were soaking, and nearly half of them were wounded. They looked a sorry state.

Hendry was shocked, but he started to help the wounded out of the flooded trenches. When they were all out and taken back from the front line to the Red Cross tents, the new soldiers took over. They had to jump into the trenches and try to get rid of the water, which was a hopeless exercise.

The enemy were quiet at first, but they were just over the brow of the hill. An hour later, all hell broke loose. Guns were firing, machine guns rattling, and bombs were hitting the trenches. They were being bombarded by the enemy.

Hendry and the other men started to fire back after they got over their first surprise, and they gave as good as they got. The battle lasted about an hour, with many wounded men lying in the trenches. The stretcher-bearers again took them back to the Red Cross camp to tend their wounds. A bullet had just grazed Hendry's head and given him a flesh wound, but he said he was fine, and wanted to stay in the trench.

Then he heard a man shouting, "Is anybody there? Hello, is anybody there?" The sound was coming from a trench further down the front line. So Hendry climbed over the trenches in between till he came to the trench where the voice was coming from. In there was a soldier who had been hurt in the arm, and he was mumbling to himself, "Neither God nor my mother is here, I am mouded wi' cull hantle.[1]" Hendry realised he was using travellers' cant.

"Are you a nakin?[2]" Hendry asked.

"Aye, I am. Thank the Lord God, he sent me another traveller."

"Are you hurt?" asked Hendry.

"Aye, but it's no' bad. It's in my arm."

Hendry helped him back to his own trench, and they sat and ate their army rations, which were a wee tin of bully beef and hard army biscuits that took you forever to eat.

They stayed in that trench for about a month, being bombarded with gunfire, bombs and hand-grenades.

One day a sergeant came running up, shouting, "Clear out,

1. I am dying among strangers   2. traveller

boys, every man for himself! The Germans are too strong for us, and we are running out of ammunition. Clear out now, and run like hell!"

So they took off and ran as fast as they could through the wood. They ran till they could run no more, and then they collapsed in a heap. There were about twenty soldiers who had stuck together. They had an hour's rest, then decided to start walking again. They could still hear gunfire away in the distance, but they were getting further away from it.

They walked on, until in front of them in the bushes they could see a white flag on a stick, waving. "I surrender," said a voice. "I give up."

Hendry listened. He knew that voice, but where did he know it from? Then it struck him. "Is that you, Wedgie?"

"Hendry, it's you!" and Wedgie ran out of the bushes and almost knocked Hendry down, he was so glad to see him. "Oh, my pal, my pal!"

"What are you doing here, Wedgie?"

"I was posted here last month, and hoped I would see you over here. All my platoon scattered. I thought you were the Germans, and I raised the white flag to surrender. Thank God it's my ain men, especially you, Hendry."

They all sat down to have another rest, and Wedgie said to them, "Anybody want a fag?"

The other men stared at him in disbelief. "Fags?" they shouted, "we ran out of them weeks ago!"

"Ah, but I have plenty." Wedgie went into the bushes and took out a small army bag, and it was full of Capstan cigarettes. "When we ran away we were at the home post, and I went to the NAAFI and took the fags."

They were happier than they had been for weeks. They must have smoked three each before they were satisfied. "What about you, Wedgie – are you no' going to have a fag?"

"I don't smoke," said Wedgie, "but I took them just in case I was taken by the enemy, and I would be able to swap them for food. But I am glad it was you boys who got them."

They started to walk again, and travelled about five miles further that day, until it was getting dark. They decided to stop to have a sleep.

Next morning Hendry got a dig in the ribs with a boot. It was British troops, who were out looking for stray soldiers. Were they pleased to see them! You can bet they were relieved that it was their own men who had found them.

The sergeant said, "It is about five miles to the coast, and we must get going, the ships are coming in at midnight to take you back to England."

They carried on following the sergeant. Wedgie was walking in front of Hendry when they heard a gunshot close by. With a quick reflex the sergeant fired up into a tree, and a German landed dead at their feet. He was a sniper.

Wedgie had been shot and was badly hurt, his guts were hanging out. Hendry ran up to him and got there first. He took him in his arms and was shouting his name, but he was dead.

They got back home without any more deaths, but Hendry had shell-shock, and was in hospital for months. He couldn't go back into the army because of the shell-shock, and he never was the same again. He stayed with his mother and father, and never married.

A Story from Ireland

I got this story from an Irish travelling family I met near Glasgow. It is set in Ireland just after the First World War.

There once was a travelling family called Sweeney who lived near Strabane in the County Tyrone. There were twelve in the family, counting the mother and father. They lived a rough life. It was very hard for all travellers in those days, never being accepted and treated like dirt by everybody. That gave them no incentive to better themselves in any way, so they just accepted what God threw at them.

This story starts round the campfire on a dark and very windy night. The fire was blowing everywhere, which made it blaze hard, and the sticks were burning too fast. There would soon be none left, and they hadn't got any before darkness came in. The father, Seán, was not too happy with his sons for not remembering to have plenty sticks at hand.

He gave them a strict telling-off to show his displeasure. The boys hung their heads in shame, because none of them wanted to get on the wrong side of their father. He was a good man, and fair, but he kept them all in order, boys and the girls as well.

There was one ragamuffin young boy among them who couldn't care less for anything, and his name was Billy. "I will go for sticks, Da," said Billy.

"You can, but not on your own, son. Michael, go with him, and don't be all night. You know the Black and Tans wander about at night, so be careful, boys."

So the boys went through the wood to fetch sticks for the fire, and Billy tripped on a tuft of grass on the ground. "Ouch, bugger me," said Billy. "I think I have done something to my ankle.

"Och, you are just saying that, to get out of gathering sticks."

"I swear on the Holy Mother above I'm not."

"I will gather the sticks, but you will have to help me carry them back to the camp."

"I will," said Billy, rubbing his ankle to try and sooth the pain away, but it didn't help much.

Michael was about half an hour away, and came back with a huge bundle of sticks. Some were rosity[1] roots that would last nearly all night on any fire. He gave Billy some, and although he was in terrible pain, he said nothing.

They got back to the camp, and were praised for bringing back so much firewood. Billy said nothing to anyone about his ankle, he just crept into bed under the bow tap wagon. That was where he slept beside his pal, the greyhound. He had a very restless night, because the pain kept him from falling asleep.

Next day his father came to wake him up. He said to his father, "I'm not feeling so well today. Can I stay in bed, Da?"

"Alright, but if you are faking I will have your hide when we come back. Kathleen, you take care of your brother."

"I will, Da."

A few hours after the rest of the family had gone away about their business, six Black and Tan soldiers came to the camp and asked if their father was there. Kathleen said no, they had gone for the day, but would be back later.

"Are you here by yourself, girl?"

"No, my brother is sick in his bed, and I'm looking after him?"

"Let me see this brother of yours."

And they lifted the cover of the wagon, but of course he wasn't there. He was underneath the wagon where his bed was. "There is no one here. Are you telling me lies, girl?"

"No, she is not. I am under here, this is where I sleep, and I am poorly today."

1. resinous

"We will make you poorly, my lad."

They dragged him out from under the wagon, and started to kick him. The blows were so painful on his sore leg, he was screaming with pain.

"Ah, we have a mammie's boy here," they said, and they kicked him another six times.

"Pain, my boy? I will show you pain of a different kind, that will make you scream for mercy. Hold him, and make him watch."

The soldier dragged Kathleen and threw her to the ground, and raped her.

"Come on now, boys, take your turn," and one after the other they molested her.

Billy was screaming like a banshee, but couldn't help his sister. After the second rape, she passed out. Then the soldiers left. Billy crawled over to her to try and see if he could help her, but it was too late, she was dead.

He was sobbing his heart out when his father came back, and when his father saw all the blood lost between the two of them, he fell to his knees, and sobbed, as did the rest of the family.

Billy told them all that had happened, and the mother put seven curses on each one of the soldiers. Kathleen was buried three days later. There was nothing that could be done about it. It was a tinker's word against theirs, and the Black and Tans always won.

Three months later Billy died with bone disease, T.B., of his leg. He was buried with his sister Kathleen in Strabane – in a field, because in these days travellers never got buried in a graveyard. The settled folk said graveyards were only for decent people.

Yes, the travellers suffered in Ireland, as well as Scotland.

Tales of Travelling Life

❧

Hawking and Fighting

A great job for travellers was tree planting. They did it for weeks on end. It was a very trying job, and back-breaking. They had to plant up hills and down hills, they never planted trees on level ground.

Peter and Mags and their son and daughter worked every year to the same man, planting trees for him. When they arrived for a new season, the man told them they wouldn't be employed that year.

"Why not?" asked Peter. "We have been coming here now for years. Why no' this year?"

"I have hired a squad o' men this year, and the work will be done faster. Sorry, Peter."

Well, they didn't know what to do. "Where will we get work now?" said Mags.

"Something will crop up, dinnae worry."

They took down their tent, bundled their belongings into a pram, and off they went.

They walked for two days till they came to Oban.

"You and the lassie will have to go telling fortunes till we get some money," said Peter.

So the women chapped the doors and told fortunes. They made about five shillings between them – enough to feed them for that day.

When they went to put up their camp, they couldn't find a place to pitch it. There were too many other travellers in the area that they didn't get on with. So they had to camp not far from a rubbish dump. They didn't like it, but there was no place else to go.

The next morning, the women went out again. After they had gone to a few houses, another traveller woman came up to them. "What do you think you are doing? This is our place to hawk. Away you go now!"

"Indeed I will not," said Mags. "You don't own this town."

The two women started to fight, and they were knocking lumps out of each other. They had a fine old scrap till the ploops[1] arrived, and the two of them were lifted.

The daughter ran all the way to the camp to tell her father that her mother was lifted with the police.

"Oh my good Lord and mercy," said Peter, "what has that woman done now?"

The three of them went down to the police station to see what was happening. When they got there, the other woman's man and her two sons were already waiting.

"I am sorry," said the policeman, "but your two wives are not getting out. They will be up in front of the judge in the morning."

"God bless me," said Peter, "that woman o' mine fights like a man."

"Ah, but so does mine," said the other traveller man.

"Well, there is nothing we can dae the night, let's go for a pint."

"That's fine, but I am barred fae every pub in the toon wi' fightin."

"Then we will get a carry-oot fae the shop," said Peter.

So off they went for whisky and beer from the shop, and went back to Peter's camp to drink it. They drank and talked, drank and talked, and had a good old time of it, and not one argument. They fell asleep at the fire.

The next morning they woke up and headed to the court house. They entered the court, which was a wee room in the

1. police

jail, and there were the two women standing before the judge. They were all ripped and torn, with black eyes, their hair standing on end as if they had jumped through a hedge backwards, and dried, caked blood on their two faces.

"God bless my soul, look at the state o' that. What did I ever see in that bap-faced woman?"

"Me too," said the other travelling man. "At least yours is a bap, mines is lantern-jawed."

The judge started to speak. "What have you got to say for yourselves? Two women fighting. What is your defence, ladies?"

"We are sorry, your lordship, but what is the meaning of the word 'defence'?"

"What can you say in your favour about the fight?" said the judge.

"Nothing," said Mags. "We had a good old scrap and enjoyed it, that's all."

"Well," said the judge, "you are both fined five shillings each, or two weeks in jail."

The two men didn't have any money to pay the fines, as they had drunk it all the night before. The two women had to stay in jail for two weeks. God help the men when they got out! I am glad I wasn't around to see it.

The Stag

Away back in the late eighteen-hundreds, travellers went in groups up into the hills of Perthshire to collect the deer horns that had been shed. They used them to make horn spoons, and various other things to sell to make a living. There were always about six tents belonging to members of the same family.

One year they got rounded up and set off on the road walking, with prams to carry their belongings. It usually took them about four or five days to arrive at the spot they wanted.

When they got there, they put up their tents and made a big fire to cook on.

The men were the ones that collected the horns, looking on the moors and in the woods and rugged fields. They never knew exactly where they would find them. So the men went away early in the morning on the first day, each with a sack to carry the horns in.

The women knew that it would be a long day for the men. It was very tiring work, with miles to travel. The women knew they would be hungry when they did come home, so they all had pots of food ready for them. Travellers (well, at least among my family) would feed the bairns first, then the wife would wait till the man came home, and share what was left between them.

The men weren't too late that night, in fact they were home before dark, because it was raining too heavily for them to look properly. However they all had some horns – not a lot, but it would keep the women working for a couple of days. The women's job was to clean the horns. Then they would get a small knife and scrape them clean, because there might be some skin left on them. They never washed them after they were

134

scraped, because water sogged them too much, and they wanted them to dry out hard. Once they had dried and they had a pile saved up, the men could work on them.

Next day the men went out again. They didn't take dogs with them, they left them at the camp, because dogs could make the deer unsettled, and the stags would try to gore the dogs. They climbed the hills and wandered many a mile, and then they sat down to rest and to have a wee blether.

"Willie," shouted John, "have you got a wee bit o' plug?[1]"

"Aye, surely. I'll halve what I have got wi' you." So they shared their pipe with each other, because there wasn't a lot of tobacco, just a pipe-full.

Suddenly Hughie stood up and said, "Boys, did you hear that rustling in the bushes just now, and snorting?"

"No' me," said John, "I heard nothing." But just then they all heard a loud snort coming from the trees. They grabbed their bags and ran down the hill, and when they looked back they saw a huge stag making up on them. They had never seen a bigger beast in all their life.

Hughie was trailing behind the other men. He wasn't as fit as the others, and was coming up in years.

Well, the stag made up on him and threw him in the air. When he came down, you could hear his leg snap, like a twig. The rest of the men stopped running and came back to help him, but they were too late. The stag gored him in the head, and it cracked open like an egg.

I tell you this exactly as it happened, because this is the way it was told to me. Travellers tell the bad and the good to their kids and keep no secrets from them, because this is a way of teaching them what life is all about. Life is hard, and was especially hard in those days for travellers.

The rest of the men managed to chase the deer away, but only after a painful thirty minutes, and all the time it was goring Hughie. When it finally stopped and ran away, they collapsed on the ground beside Hughie, or what was left of him, and they

1. tobacco

burst into tears.

Hughie had three bairns, two girls and a wee boy. What were they going to tell his wife, Mary? They decided to bury him there and then. They could not take him home in the state he was in. Together they all dug a hole very deep, and one of the men drew his jacket over him when he was in the hole. Then they filled the hole in. They lifted his bag of horns and made for the tents.

John said it was the saddest day of his life, having to tell Mary that Hughie was dead. The women all gathered round to comfort her, but she went to bed the saddest woman alive.

The next morning, the men said they would take Mary to Hughie's grave. They were all sitting round the fire, the men, the women and the kids. Mary thanked everybody for being so kind to her, but no, she said, she didn't want to see the grave. "He is gone now, and what would be the use? I am going back to my mother and father. I will give my father the horns Hughie lost his life over, and he can use them. My parents will help me bring up my wains. I won't see you again next year, but we'll meet again at some camping spot or another."

The other travellers said goodbye to Mary and the bairns. They never went back to that glen ever again. It was insantifit.[1]

1. unlucky, cursed

Education of the Traveller

People think the travelling people have no education. But there is more to education than being able to read and write. Travellers need to learn about survival; about work (making things to sell – basket-making, horn spoon-making); how to build their own houses (bow tents); hawking; pearl-fishing; drukkering (reading fortunes); how to look after a horse if you have money to buy one; how to light and keep going an outside fire. Or if you build a gelly (two bow tents put together) for the winter months, how to make a fire out of a big drum can, with a chimney.

Many, many years ago there was a spot in Perthshire where all the travellers met to teach their kids these skills. It was up at Prosen above Kirriemuir. They would get their kids together, girls as well as boys, when they arrived, and make them put up their bow tents.

They were watched by their parents, or other travellers, and were guided in how to build them. Sometimes they got into a fankle, but they would be shown the proper way, how to bow the sticks, how to tie them, sometimes with heather, and how to place the cover over them, and get big stones to hold the cover down.

There was one wee boy, named after his grandfather, who was called for a nickname Moaskins, which means tiny. He was four years old, and wanted to join in everything the rest were doing. So his father told him to watch how it was done and he would let him build a small bow tent for his dog, Terry. He was over the moon at being allowed to take part. He watched carefully when they were bowing the sticks, and he did it just as they did, but he had no cover to put over them, and he started to cry.

"Wheesht now, my laddie, we will think of something for you." So his father got an old sack, opened it out, and the wee boy was over the moon with it.

The parents would inspect the tents to see if they were done right. Then they would show the kids how to light a fire to make their habbin.[1] After they were shown, the women made the habbin, and that was the lessons over for the day. They all went to their own tents and were fed.

Moaskins came greeting to his mother, saying, and crying at the same time, "Terry won't go into the tent I made for him, why not?"

His mother made him eat his supper first, and promised she would go and see what the problem was, if he ate everything up, after the dishes were done by the lassies.

Moaskins and his mother went to see what was wrong with Terry, and why he wouldn't go into the wee bow tent that was made for him. His mother looked in and said, "What is this you have put in here?"

"Nothing," said the boy.

"Well," said the mother, "there is something in there now, and the smell is choking me to death."

Moaskins poked his head through the cover of the tent, and said, "What's that smell, mither?"

"Shite," said his mother. "Div you no ken the smell o' shite when you smell it?"

"Yuk, yuk!" said the boy. "Who done that?"

"It will be them boys again, playing a practical joke on you."

The boy ran home and told his father.

"Well," said the father, "you have learned two lessons today – putting up a bow-tent, and learning to be a boy and take a joke. You will have to clean the tent yourself, or they have won."

"No way have they won!"

So Moaskins tore down the tent, and put it up in another spot, much cleaner. Then he went and pulled grass and cleaned

1. food

138

up the mess that was in the tent. He was being watched by two other wee boys. They came out and said sorry to him, it was them that had done it, and they helped him clean it up, so they were pals again. Terry went straight into the tent and fell asleep. Moaskins thought, "My Daddy was right. I have learned through this."

Next day they started to make baskets and horn spoons. They all went and collected the wands to make the baskets, and picked some of the warer[1] in the river, and made a big pool like a dam, to put the wands in to soak overnight.

Then all the young ones sat round in a circle to watch the horn spoon being made. The girls cleaned the outside by scraping it with a rough stone. Then they handed it to the boys to be instucted how to clean the inside of the horn, and to scrape out the marrow. After that they got a very hot wire to poke into it to burn off anything that was left inside. Then they took a big knife, stuck it in the fire, measured the horn in lengths, and burned it through with the knife. They scraped the burned marks off to clean the horn, and put it aside to dry out completely. That was the lesson for the day, and the kids could go away and play and enjoy themselves.

Moaskins' pals came up to him to play. "What will we play at?" asked Moaskins.

"We ken what we are going to do, but maybe you won't like it."

"Tell me, then, what is it?"

"We are going to follow the lassies tae see how they sloosh.[2]"

"Yuk," said Moaskins, "that's wild. Why are you going to do that?"

"Cause they don't stand up like we do."

"Aye, they do so. My ma does, she just stands and lets it flee fae her."

"Well, if you don't want to come, you can stay, but we are going."

1. reeds   2. pee

"Alright, I'll go wi' you, but just to prove you wrong," said Moaskins.

So off they went and hid among the bushes in the wood till they heard the lassies coming. They kept very quiet, and watched the lassies as they stopped and looked around. Then the lassies all squatted down, and the boys could hear it coming from them. The boys then ran away as fast as they could, before they were discovered.

Near bedtime that night, Moaskins was sitting awful quiet. "What's wrong wi' you, my wee laddie," asked his father. "Did you learn anything today?"

"Well, maybe. I saw lassies slooshing, and they sat doon tae dae it." His father burst out laughing. "Well, you certainly learned something, my wain, and you'll have more to come as you get older!" He was still laughing as he went to bed.

Things started early the next morning, because they were to make baskets. It wasn't just a learning thing for the kids, it was to make stock to sell as well. They all went down to the river, got the wands from the pool, and carried them up to the camp. The adults showed them how to peel the bark in separate pieces at the top like a banana. Then they wrapped the peeled bits round the cane and pulled them down, and that stripped the bark off. The young ones watched with eyes glued to what they were doing. Then they started to do it themselves, with the eagerness of any young person wanting to learn a trade. When the bark was all off, which took them a few hours, they then used a cleave, a tool for splitting the cane down the middle into many pieces. There were only three of the men that had a cleave, which they had made for themselves.

Once they knew how to do the basic preparation, the kids started to learn how to make baskets: hawking baskets, turly[1] baskets, skulls which were sold to farmers for the tatties, small square baskets and many more. They learned to do this job well. Because it took them a week to finish all the baskets, they had a lot of time to learn to make their own. Even wee Moaskins

1. round

was taught, but couldn't do it very well, because he was too young yet.

The next day the boys were taken down to the river to learn pearl-fishing. They had ten glass jugs they made themselves, so they could look down in the water. These were made out of a luggy[1] with the bottom taken out. They got glass in the shape of the bottom of the bucket, and they placed the glass in the bottom against the rim they had left in the bucket. This was then sealed with candle grease, and when the bucket was put in the water the candle grease hardened, so never a drop of water got through. They also had ten long sticks they had cut off the trees that morning, with one end shaped like a clothes peg, and they used these to get the shells out of the water.

At the same time the girls would be with the women being taught the drookering (reading hands, or tea-cups). It probably was a good thing to learn, but my family wasn't into telling fortunes, so it isn't something I was taught.

So there was a lot of learning going on. It was the travellers' trade to learn these things. So who is to say that the traveller wasn't educated? You had to learn ways of surviving when you weren't accepted by non-travellers. They often think that because we had no formal education and didn't learn to read and write we must be stupid. But we do have knowledge, and common sense, and no one can take that away from us.

Years after this, wee Moaskins grew up to be a big strong man, and he was the best basket-maker in his day in Perthshire.

1. small bucket

The Flax

There was a farmhouse about eight miles from Dundee, and it took in travellers to help with pulling the flax. There would be about five tents there, and maybe it would take them about three weeks to pull all the flax. One year only one of the families that usually came was there. The farmer didn't know the rest, but they were tinks, and would do a good job. To give them time to settle in, they arrived on a Sunday to start work on the Tuesday.

The family that had been going there for years, a man, a wife, three sons and two daughters, were a wee bit wary of the rest of the travellers who had come, as they didn't know much about them. The new families came from away up north in the Caithness area. They were civil enough, but there was something about them that the man of the family didn't trust. He couldn't put his finger on it. They seemed to be too quiet for his liking. They even asked what flax was, and what was made from it. Well, the traveller man explained to them that flax was a surface plant, very easy to pull, and it went to make linseed oil.

They accepted what he told them, but found it difficult to understand. They didn't seem very keen to learn, it was as if they couldn't care less what they did. "As long as it's work, we will do it," one of the men said.

The new women weren't allowed to speak to the woman who had been coming for years, they kept themselves to themselves. The newcomers were all of the same family, all four tents – brothers, sisters, cousins, grannies and grandas, men and wives.

Tuesday morning arrived, and they had to start at eight o'clock. By eight-thirty there was no sign of the new people.

142

Nine o'clock came and at last they turned up for work. The farmer wasn't too pleased with them, but because they hadn't done the job before, he let them off with it this time.

"How do we do the job?" they asked the farmer.

"Well, Jimmy here will teach you, and show you what to dae," the farmer said. Jimmy was the travelling man who had been coming to the same farm for years.

So Jimmy showed them what to do, and they worked well till twelve o'clock. Then Jimmy called for them to stop, because it was dinner time. So they all rushed back to their tents, went in, closed the tent doors and they all fell asleep without eating anything.

Jimmy thought this very strange, as did his wife. At the end of the day they all went back to the tents, and again they went straight into their tents and put down the cover over the doors.

Jimmy said to his wife, "I can't stand this, I must find out what's wrong with them."

So over he went to the door of the tent and shouted to the man that he wanted to speak to him. So out he came, and Jimmy said to him, "Why do you all go into your tents without making a fire to make yourselves any food? I am sorry for asking you, but that's three days now we haven't seen you eat. Not even a cup of tea did you make. I ken it's none of my business, but I am wondering why."

"Well, to tell you the truth, and I am embarrassed about it, that is why we are hiding. We have no money to buy food, and it is three days since we had anything to eat."

"Oh my God," said Jimmy, "how did you no' tell us sooner? We haven't much, but we could have shared it with you."

"No, no," said the man, whose name was Jock, "there are too many of us – four tents full."

"Come wi' me," said Jimmy, and he took him up to the farm and had a word with the farmer.

"My goodness," said the farmer, "I didn't know you hadn't eaten for three days! Here –" and he gave him five pounds.

"Oh my good God almighty, it's a long time since I saw a five pound note."

"You and your family have earned it," said the farmer.

"But no' all that amount."

"Well, no," said the farmer, "but I will no' take it off all at once. I'll spread it over the next three weeks, alright?"

"It's more than alright," said Jock, with his chest sticking out and holding his head up high, and his waistcoat was fit to burst with pride and thankfulness.

They got back to the tents. Jock shouted to his wife to come out and showed her the five pound note. Her two eyes were bolting out of her head.

"Where did you get that?" his wife asked.

"Well," said Jock, "Jimmy took me up to the farmer, and he gave it to me as a sub."

"You mean we can buy habbin¹ now?"

"Yes, we can. Get your shawl and we will awa tae the shop."

He shouted to one of his laddies to go get some sticks, and shouted to the lassie to go for a bucket of water, and have the kettle boiling. "We are going to eat tonight, thank God. No – thanks to Jimmy," and away they went to the shops. One of the other women went with them as well.

Jimmy and his wife put on a big sloorach,² and soon were fed. Then Jock and his wife and the other woman came back. They were loaded down with shopping. Their fire was blazing and the kettle was boiling. The women had a pot boiling for the tatties already, because the farmer had given them a few bags that day. There were three women peeling them and the pot was reaming full and boiling away nicely.

Jimmy and his wife turned their back on the family when they were eating because they didn't want to be looking in their faces, that was ignorant. Eventually Jock came over to Jimmy and said, "Now, Jimmy, I feel great and I'm farting full."

"That's great, Jock, but I want to ask you something. There

1. food   2. stew

was more wrong with youse than not having food, am I right?"

Jock hung his head, and started to shake it. "Oh dear, aye there is. My laddie was killed last week up in Caithness. He got battered to death with two ploughmen, and they told us to get out of there, and not to tell the police. So we had to pack up and go. I had to protect the rest o' my family. We went and said nothing, and buried my laddie on the way down here."

Jimmy knew what the country hantle[1] were like – their word was taken before any traveller's.

"Aye, the ploughmen can be coarse, alright, and they are big and hefty men. You did the right thing, Jock."

"Well, I hope so, because we cannae go back up there again. We will have to stay down here."

"I am sure once you get used to it, youse will all be fine."

They went to work the next day as usual, but Jimmy kept looking at wee Annie, his middle daughter. She wouldn't take her eyes off Jock's son, Frankie. He was a fine-looking boy, but he was small like Annie was. Annie was four feet ten, and Frankie would be about five feet nothing. He was always keeking[2] at Annie as well. Jimmy thought to himself they would make a fine couple, but said nothing to anyone.

Annie was late coming home for her supper that night, after work, and Jimmy noticed Frankie wasn't there either. An hour later, Annie turned up, with her face like a beetroot, and she was boiling with rage. She would eat nothing, and ran into her tent.

"Well, well," thought Jimmy, "what's up here?" So he went into the tent after her.

"What's wrong wi' you, my doll?"

"It's him," she said "Frankie. We went for a walk after work, across the fields, and we sat doon, and he asked me to take my knickers aff. Some cheek, wasn't it, Da? And he kept touching my pappies[3] and stroking my legs. So I slapped him and ran home. Did I do the right thing, Da?"

1. non-travellers   2. glancing   3. breasts

"Yes, my doll, you did. I must have a word wi' his father about this."

Jimmy went over to Jock's tent and called him out. They sat down on the grass, and Jimmy told him what Annie had said. Jock started to foam at the mouth with anger. "Now see here, Jimmy, my laddie wouldn't dae that."

"But he did. My Annie is not a liar. She wouldn't say that if it wasn't true."

"Right," said Jock. "We will get the two thegither, and get the truth oot o' them."

"Fine wi' me," said Jimmie.

They got hold of them, and made them sit down round the fire, and asked them what had happened.

All Frankie would say was, "I want her, I want her."

The men sat with a smile on their face, and then they turned to Annie, glaring at her. They asked if she wanted to say anything.

"Well," said Annie, "I like him, I like him a lot, if he would stop groping my pappies so much."

"Alright," said Frankie, "I winna grope you."

Jock gave a smile, and said to Jimmy, "Well, Jimmy, if God made them, he matched them."

"Yes, I agree wi' you, Jock."

So they were told to go away for a week, and when they came back they would be man and wife. No man would touch a soiled woman, that's what they thought in those days. No marriages, just go away, and when they came back, in the eyes of the families they would be man and wife. The fathers gave them some money and an old cover to make a tent, and away they went for a week. While they were away, the fathers built them a good bow tent with plenty of room in it for when they came back.

Now one of Jimmy's laddies was eying up Jock's daughter Meg. She was a sour-faced lassie, and awful quiet. One night he came home after going a walk with her, and told his father that he had had his way with her.

"*What!*" said Jimmy, "are you telling me you did it with her?"

"No, don't be silly. She let me grope her, and she liked it, and so did I."

"What am I going to do with my family, they are all sex mad! I must go again and tell Jock our wains are moich.[1]"

"Well, we have no money left to send them away. So we will have to give them the tent we built for Frankie and Annie, and we can build another one for them when they come back."

They had a word with the mothers, and they had to agree. Then they sent for the couple, and told them. They agreed, and moved in together that night.

After the flax was over, they had a few pounds to come for the farmer. Jock shared it out among his folk, and so did Jimmy.

They all stuck together after that, and worked together, and became the best of friends. They had their ups and downs, and their arguments, and fights as well when they had a dram, which wasn't very often, just now and again. I can't say they lived happy ever after, because this is travellers we are speaking about, and they had their troubles with the country hantle[2] as all travellers did. But they were happy enough.

1. daft   2. non-travellers

The Market

This is a story I got from a travelling woman many years ago. It was relatives of hers that were hanged in the story about Willie Duff.

There was always a market in Blairgowrie in the summer time. It was held at the Well Meadow, and it was for travellers to deal in horses. It always attracted a lot of the Blairgowrie folk who were not travellers. It was on every Saturday, all day.

One market day a traveller brought a mare. It was a superb beast, prancing around as if it owned the place, and it caught the attention of a farmer.

"Oh my God, that is some horse," he said. "I would die for a horse like that, and that's no kidding."

He shouted to his tractor driver, and also to his son, Willie, "Come here a minute!"

His son came over and said, "What do you want, Dad?"

"Look at that mare over there, prancing about."

His son couldn't believe his eyes as he gazed on the mare. "Goodness me," said the boy, "it is a great horse, are you going to buy it?"

"Can you see me no' buying it?" said the farmer. He walked up to the man who was leading the horse round.

"How much you want for the mare?"

"This is a travellers' market, and you are no' a traveller."

"Does it matter? My money is just the same as travellers' money."

"No, I cannae sell it to you," said the traveller.

"I will give you double of what any traveller can give you."

"I would like to take your money, but I can't do it," answered the traveller, and he walked away with the horse.

148

He didn't sell it to anyone else, he was in too big a hurry to get away.

"Something's wrong," thought the farmer to himself. "I will find out what."

He turned round and said to his tractor man, "Find out where that tinker man with the horse has his camp." So the tractor man went off, and the farmer went to the pub for a drink. His son went with him.

He said to his son, "The tractor man is away to find out where that tinker man has his tent, maybe we can change his mind and get him to sell us the horse."

"You are really set on getting that mare, aren't you Dad?"

"Yes," said the farmer. "I fell in love with it as soon as I saw it. I must have it."

The traveller man stayed at the Ponfaulds, and was picking berries at Park Hill. When he got back to his tent, his old mother was there. "Well, son, how did you get on at the market?"

"No' so good, mother. I sold the pony, but the travellers had not enough money to buy the mare. Maybe at the end o' the berries they will have saved enough to buy it, God knows."

His old mother was blind. She hadn't always been blind, but she lost her sight when she was about thirty. She had a funny thing happen to her a few weeks after she lost her sight. She could smell colours. Yes, smell colours. It was an amusement for the rest of the travellers at the camp, because she would do it for them. Jean was her name.

"Sit doon, son and I will give you habbin.[1]"

Now, back at the pub, the farmer was waiting on his tractor man coming back. In he came, and told the farmer where the traveller's tent was.

"Right," said the farmer, "we will go and have a crack wi' them." So off he went to the campsite. He looked for the mare and found it, and that showed where the tent was.

They came to the fire, and the traveller man looked up and

1. food

saw it was the man who wanted to buy his horse. "What are you doing here?" he asked the farmer.

"Well, I have come to see if you have changed your mind about selling the mare to me."

"What's this?" said the old woman. "You said you never got an offer for the mare!"

"Excuse me, sir, while I speak to my mother in private," the traveller said to the farmer, and they went into the tent.

"Nasemort, you jan I cannae bing the grie tae country hantle. You jan it's chored." ("Mother, you know I can't sell the horse to this man, because you know it is stolen.")

"How much did the coul mang he would bing ye for the grie?" ("How much did he offer you for it?")

"He said twice the money any nakin[1] would give me for it."

"Right, leave it to me, I have an idea," said the mother.

They came out of the tent, and sat round the fire, where the farmer was waiting.

"Well," said the auld woman, "you want to buy wir mare?"

"Yes, I do," said the farmer.

"Well, there is a condition connected wi' it," said old Jean. "How much will you give us for the mare, is my first question."

"A good price," said the farmer.

"How much?" asked the old woman.

"Twenty pounds," was the farmer's answer.

Now twenty pounds was a lot of money then, but Jean said, "If you make it thirty, I might think aboot it, but there is a trick to getting the mare. I am stone blind as you can see, but I can smell colours. Son, bring me my hankies."

So the son went into the tent, and took out the coloured hankies. There was every colour of the rainbow.

"Now," said Jean, and she threw the hankies on the grass. "You can pick the colours, and let me smell them."

She sat there with a wee smile on her face. "Now, if I make a mistake," she said, "you can have the mare for thirty pounds,

1. traveller

150

and if I win, we keep the mare and you still give us thirty pounds."

The farmer thought to himself, no way can she smell colours. "Very well," said the farmer, "I agree."

He picked up a hanky and let her smell it. "It's pink," she said.

"Yes, you are right," said the farmer. He picked up another one.

"Oh, that's green," she said.

"Right again," said the farmer, wondering if he had made the right decision to agree to her bet.

She went on in the same way for another six times, and was correct every time.

The next hanky he picked up was black. "White!" shouted the old woman.

The farmer's heart began to flutter. "You are wrong," said the farmer. "I won the horse!"

"Aye," the old woman replied, "but you have to give me thirty pounds, and you must promise never to tell anybody where you bought the mare. If you do, a tinker's curse will follow you all your days."

The farmer agreed, and went away with the mare he so desperately wanted to possess.

"Well," said the old woman to her son, "I got you out of that mess, and got you thirty pounds as well."

"How is that good?" her son asked her.

"Well, think aboot it, laddie. No country hantle[1] would ever cross a tinker, because they are feared o' the tinker's curse, and you got rid of the horse, and we gained thirty pounds. You cannae get done for it being chored.[2] If anybody is going to be in trouble it will be the farmer, and he won't say a word about how he came by it. He will just say he bought it off a tinker at Blairgowrie horse market. All he will lose is his thirty pounds, and the mare taken from him, he winnae get the quod.[3]"

It was a successful berry season for Jean and her son that year.

---

1. non–traveller   2. stolen   3. jail

Travellers' Hobbies

There is not enough told about the travellers' hobbies, as people would call them nowadays. They did have hobbies, outwith their hawking. At night when they were relaxing back at the camp they did various things to pass the time. This is a story about a family who did just that.

This story starts in the year 1930, in a place called Struan in Perthshire. It is about a family who travelled a lot, and always stayed at Struan in the wintertime. They were Stewarts. This year they had pitched their tent in the usual place, and got themselves settled in for the winter.

They were all sitting round the fire one night, when one of the boys spoke up. "Well, I don't ken aboot you yins, but this winter isn't going to be wasted by me. I am going to teach myself something."

"What for?" asked the father.

"To pass the time, especially when the snow comes, and we are hemmed in here. It would be good having something to take wir minds aff the winter."

"Have you thocht what you are going tae dae?"

"Yes, I have. I am going to learn myself how to draw."

"Draw! What benefit is that going tae dae ye, silly laddie?"

"You never ken, Da, but I am going tae try it."

The next day he went to the shop, and he just had enough money to buy some blank bits of paper. After supper that night, he got the paper out, and spread it in front of him. He leaned forward to the fire, and took a black ember out of it, and waited till it was cool. Then he started to draw on the paper.

Within the next few days he drew everything in sight, getting better all the time. He had no pencil, but just sketched with the charcoal out of the fire.

One night they were all sitting down, and his father said to him, "Are you no' drawing the night then, laddie?"

"I have nothing left to draw, I have drawn everything in sight."

"Well," said the father, "Why don't you start on nature? There is plenty of that around here."

"That's a bliddy good idea, Da. I will."

So he wandered about, drawing trees, weeds, heather and gorse. That gave him great pleasure and satisfaction as well. Then he started on animals and birds. He was, by this time, a great drawer, and everyone in the camp praised him for it.

"How can we no' think of something to dae as well?" said his sister. Jean was her name.

"What would you want to do, Jean?" her brother Doddie asked her.

"You will laugh at me if I tell you, Doddie."

"No, I won't. Tell me."

"I want to learn the pipes."

"A lassie playing the pipes? I have never seen a woman piper," said Doddie.

"No, and maybe you never will, but I would like to try."

"Da has an auld chanter lying aboot somewhere, I will get it for you."

"They will all laugh at me, but I ken I have it in me, and I can do it."

"That's a' you need, like me, a wee bit push. Go for it, Jean! I will no' tell anybody till you are able to play a tune. You can go doon by the burn, and nobody will hear you with the noise of the river running."

"Oh me, Doddie, you are a godsend tae me. I have wanted to do this all my life. I used to get a bit stick and kiddie on it was a chanter."

"Nae mair kiddie on, Jean, you will do it."

The next day Doddie came to her, and signalled to her to

follow him. They walked down to the burn, and he took the chanter out of his jacket and handed it to her.

"Oh dear me, and the blissens o' God, you got it for me!"

"I telt you I would."

She examined it in her hand, and turned to her brother. "God, dear, it's a Hardie's chanter."

"What does that mean, Jean?"

"It's the maker's name that made it."

"How do you ken that?"

"There's things aboot me youse don't know. I ken mair than I let on, Doddie boy."

Time wore on, and they had been there two months. Jean slipped away every chance she got to practice. Doddie didn't have to hide, because they all knew he drew.

Now Ecky, the other brother, was getting gey lonely with nobody to speak to or hang about with. He walked up to Doddie one night, and said, "Doddie, what can I dae to pass the time? I am wearied."

"I ken the very thing for you, Ecky, and I will make one for you."

They went through the wood and found a willow bush. Doddie got a stick off it, sat down with his wee pocket knife, scraped the soft inside out of it, and made it as clean as a piece of pipe. Then he carved holes in it, shaped a mouthpiece, and there before Ecky's eyes was a whistle.

"Now," said Doddie, "learn yourself to play it." Ecky was over the moon, and said he was going to be at it all the time, till he mastered it.

That was three happy bairns, with each of them having a hobby, but they never knew at that time that's what it was called. They thought it was just to pass the time and not be bored.

This went on for another month, and it was getting near to the New Year and Hogmanay. The two bairns were practising together now, to make a surprise for their mam and dad, with the chanter and the whistle played together.

Doddie decided to make cards for every one, personal ones. He drew one of his father, to give to his mother, and one of his mother to give to his father. He made a bird one for Jean, and a horse for Ecky. The cards were so beautiful.

They were sitting round the fire, and it was a quarter to twelve, nearly midnight. Ecky slipped away, then Jean slipped away. When they thought it was about twelve o'clock, Doddie said, "Happy New Year, Ma and Da," and the two came in to the fire, playing the chanter and the whistle. Doddie has hopping and skipping about like a cull.[1] Their mother and father's faces were a pleasure to see, they couldn't believe it. They all said "Happy New Year" to each other, and they had a half-bottle to celebrate.

They eventually sat round the fire tired and weary. "Now," said the father, "Your mither will sing for you."

"Oh John, I cannae. I haven't sang for years."

"Oh yes, you will. If our bairns can do it, so can you, wee woman."

So she started to sing:

> "Bonny wee thing, canny wee thing,
> Bonny wee thing, thing of mine."

Her voice rang out through the night air, and lingered even when she had finished singing. There was a great peace came over the camp that night, because they all felt they had succeeded in something to pass the time. The only thing the father succeeded in was emptying the half-bottle, and being proud of his family.

That's the last New Year they spent together. That year they were all drowned in the Caledonian Canal.

1. silly person

The Forge

Many, many years ago, travelling people in the winter-time followed the forge. Blacksmiths and farmers had forges, where the travellers would go to make their tin ready to be sold in the summertime. Usually they had the same forges year after year that they went to. My great-great-grandfather, Elijah, went to a farmer's forge every year. This story begins about the year 1870. It's about a mishap that happened at one of these forges.

A travelling family turned up one day to a forge in the south of Scotland. They hadn't been to a forge before, but were great tinsmiths. They came from just over the borders in England. They were a family that had done something wrong in Scotland in the past, and so had stayed away from the country for a lot of years. The old man had done the wrong, but it was now his son, and his wife and kids that were travelling in Scotland. The son said to his wife they would be safe now, because his father had died.

The forge they came to was in Dumfriesshire. They approached the man who owned the forge, and asked him if they could stay for the winter and use his forge. The blacksmith agreed, because the travellers that used to come to him had moved away a few years back. So he welcomed them, but he said they could only stay for a month, and no longer. They agreed to this, and settled down for the month, and put their tents up.

Now this family's name was Livingston. The man's name was Roddy and the wife's name was Ann. They had two sons, Charlie and Hector.

They had one daughter too – her name was Jean, and she was aged fourteen. She was deaf in one ear, born that way, and she was the clumsiest creature on God's earth. She was sensible enough, but accidents – she could have won hands down to anybody. For instance, if her mother asked her to put water in the kettle for tea, she would spill the whole bucketful of water on the ground, and none would get in the kettle. She tripped one day, and pushed her mother into the river by accident. And snore – she could snore for Scotland. Her life was a disaster. That is why her mother and father kept a close eye on her, and for the same reason she was barred from the forge.

One day, when everyone was away, she was told to look after the camp till her mother came home from the shop. She tidied up, and then went for a walk. She had been told not to move from the camp, but did she heed? No!

She strolled across a field, where she saw some peewits, and she thought to herself, "If that's peewheeps, there will be eggs there." Travellers loved peesies' eggs (that's what the travellers called them – peesies and peewheeps). So she went across the field looking for them, and found six.

Now Jean was feart of everything, and when one of the pee-wheeps flew over her head, she ran into a wee wooded clearing, and started to climb a tree to get away from the bird, but she missed her footing and fell. She fell right into a cow's bap,[1] all the eggs got broken, and they ran down her frock. The eggs were rotten ones, and the smell was terrible.

She started to cry, and tried to find her way home, but it was getting dark. In the end she got back alright, but what a mess she was in.

"Oh my God," said her mother when she saw her, "what have you been up to, Jean? Look at you, you thickent[2] lassie."

Her mother caught her by the hair, took her to the river and pushed her in. She got her by the scruff of the neck and washed her in the stream till she was spotless clean. Then she dragged her home and told her to go to her bed in case she took the cold, because it was a frosty day and very bitter.

1. cow pat   2. daft

The next morning, Ann, the mother, took ill after Roddy and the boys had gone to the forge. She was doubled up with cramps, and told Jean to go up to the forge to fetch Roddy.

"But I cannae go, I am banned from the forge," said Jean.

"I cannae help it, you have to go and fetch yer father. I need him."

So off Jean ran to get her father. She scrambled into the forge shouting her head off and tripped, knocking the farmer towards the burning forge. He put out his hand to save himself from falling, and his hand went into the burning coals. Roddy grabbed him and pulled him back, but his hand was on fire. The boys ran and got a bucket of water and put the farmer's hand into the bucket. The farmer was in a terrible state. One of the farmhands jumped on his horse and went for the doctor.

An hour later the doctor arrived and looked at the hand. "I am sorry," said the doctor, "but the hand must come off. It is too charred, and the nerves are all burned, and so are the sinews. Take him outside, men, and I will whip it off. Hurry, we must not delay!"

So they carried the farmer outside and laid him down at the door of the forge. The doctor took a big axe that was hanging up and doused it with whisky from his hip flask. Then he got a big log, put the hand on the log, and told the men to hold the farmer down while he cut it off. He gave one swing of the axe, and plunk! – the hand was cut clean off from the arm, and the blood went everywhere.

"Hold him down, boys, this next thing is going to sting like mad!"

They got a good grip of him, and the doctor poured whisky on the stump. A murder roar came out of the farmer. He was in agony, and he passed out with the pain.

"Now," said the doctor, "tell me exactly what happened."

The men told the doctor what happened, that it was Jean that pushed him towards the forge, and his hand had gone in.

"Well, you know," said the doctor, "I have to report this to the police."

Roddy looked up in fear. "The police!" he thought. "They will take wee Jean away from us, for good, and we won't ever see her again."

He grabbed his daughter's hand, and he and the boys went back to the camp. He told Ann the minute he got back, and said they would have to get away quick, before the feekies[1] arrived. Ann was feeling a lot better, and told them she was alright. Her pains were because she was with child, and the pain had gone now.

They all packed up and left, and headed towards England again. They hid in the bushes during the day, and travelled all night, and the next day in the afternoon they reached Carlisle. Like Roddy's father, they never dared go back to Scotland ever again.

1. police

Orphanages

Another very bad thing that happened to the travellers long ago was that the children would be taken from the travellers and put in a home for orphans. Even people in my family, long, long ago, were taken away.

There was a family that stayed just outside Dundee. There was a man, a wife and their six kids. Then the wife had died. The authorities said he couldn't look after the young children without a woman to help, even though one of the girls was seventeen. Five of them were taken away and put into an orphanage. The girl of seventeen was left with her father, who died of a broken heart two years later.

§

One year the authorities swooped down on a group of travellers and were going to take all their kids away. One woman's husband had died, and they said she couldn't look after her children by herself without a man. They told her they were coming the next day to take them into a home.

That night the woman got her kids together and ran away, carrying the wee one on her back. She had four children altogether, three boys and one girl. The girl was the eldest.

They wandered for a few days begging food here and there from other travellers. They were afraid to put up a tent in case they would be found out and the police would come. They slept among the bushes or in a wood. They slept out in all weathers – sun, rain, and wind. The authorities treated them like runaway slaves, not human beings.

After a week she was caught. The kids went into a home, and she was put in jail. She got six months for running away, and never saw her kids again. She went mad and died in a mental institution.

§

When travellers' kids were taken from them, it was terrible, it played with their minds. A lot of the older children were sent to the colonies to supply workers for mines and other places. It was not just men who were sent down the mines, boys were made to work there as well. They disappeared, never to be seen again. It wasn't just non-travellers who were transported to the colonies. Many travellers were as well.

The Poacher's Dog

I got this story from a man in a pub up north. He was drinking a pint at the time, but I don't think he was drunk – at least he said he wasn't.

I was a wee laddie at the time this happened. It was at a campsite up north of here. We were on the site about a week when the poacher arrived – that's what everybody called him, because that's how he made his money. He had a greyhound named Punter, and he had taught Punter to dive into the water and fetch out salmon. He was the biggest show-off, and none of the travellers liked to stay beside him, because of his bumming. He always showed off about never being caught by the police or the water bailiff.

He put his tent up, and the first thing he did was to feed his dog. He had boiled a rabbit the day before, he told us, and he fed the dog what was left of it.

He made a fire, fed himself and sat round it playing a Jew's harp. This was annoying, because he only knew one tune, and kept playing it over and over again. It was getting on the other travellers' nerves.

Big Sam went over to him, caught him by the throat and said, "Enough is enough." He grabbed the Jew's harp from him and threw it on the fire. "Now we will get peace," said Big Sam. The poacher said nothing, because no one argued with Big Sam, but he thought to himself, "My fire is low, and my Jew's harp won't burn, because it's not wood, it's metal. I can get it back in the morning."

The next day the poacher went away about ten o'clock, and he came back at three whistling away to himself, and a smile all over his face.

"Well, and how did you get on today, poacher?" said my father.

"O fine, just fine. I made a bundle today off the folk in the village pubs, buying my salmon. Yes, it was a very good day for me, I must say. I must go and feed my dog now."

Later on I was going to my bed, when I heard a Jew's harp playing away in the distance, down by the river. I sneaked down and followed the music. When I got close the music stopped and I heard voices. It was the poacher and a travelling girl from the camp called Sally. I could hear he was trying to court her. She was about seventeen, and I thought she was far too young for the poacher. I interrupted them and said her father was looking for her. Sally ran back to the camp like a frightened cat, but at least I got her away from him.

A few days later it was a Saturday, and that's when all the men went to the pub. They drank all day Saturday till about five o'clock, then they came home, because they didn't want to be there when the villagers came in.

My father told us later that day what happened in the pub that afternoon, and he was laughing as he told us. They were all in the pub, and so was the poacher, drinking away. The police came in to see if all was well as they always do. At that very moment, what should come through the door but the poacher's dog, and in his mouth was a big salmon. Everyone started to laugh, and the policeman noticed the dog and came over to the poacher. "Is this your dog?"

The poacher was chatting and never noticed the salmon at his feet. "Yes, it is my dog, is he not allowed in a pub?"

"Yes, he is, but not when he is poaching a salmon. Up you get and come down to the police station with me, you're under arrest." The poacher went away with his tail between his legs, and head bent.

He got three months, and his dog was taken from him and given to the dogs' home. Three months later he got out, and the last we heard, he had run away with Sally.

Tragic and Comic Stories

❧

The Shock

There was a traveller man and woman, and they had two kids. The man's name was Moosie, and the woman's name was Belle. The wee boy was called Jamie, and for a nickname the wee lassie was called Winkins. Jamie was five, and Winkins was just three. They were a family who kept themselves to themselves, and didn't camp near other travellers. The parents were over-protective of the two bairns. They had to play where they could be seen at all times.

They had their supper one night late, and decided to go to bed, because they were tired with hawking all day. Through the middle of the night came a great storm, pouring down rain. Moosie and Belle never heard a thing, but when they awoke early the next morning, they were flooded out, everything was drenched.

"Are you alright, Jamie?"

"Yes, Daddy, I am fine, just soakin."

"Winkins, are you there?" No answer.

"Winkins!" Moosie shouted again. Still no answer.

By this time Belle had started to scream, shouting her daughter's name, and wee Jamie was greeting for his wee sister. They ran outside, and searched everywhere, shouting all the while. But she wasn't anywhere to be seen. They all collapsed in a heap together, hugging each other for comfort.

"What will we do now?" said Belle, between sobs.

"We will have to go and see the police, and report her missing. Maybe they have picked her up already."

"Do you think maybe they have?"

"We won't know till we get down there. Come on then, let's get moving."

With heavy hearts they walked down to the police station. Moosie said to the constable, "We have lost our little girl, is she here?"

"What would she be doing here?" asked the policeman.

"Well, you see we woke up this morning and she was gone. We never heard the rain through the night, and she must have wandered away during it."

"How old is she?" asked the policeman.

"She is only three," said Belle, crying all the time.

"Your kind o' folk shouldn't be allowed to have bairns, when you canny look after them properly. Awa' ye go, and don't waste my time looking for your bastard bairns."

So they left the police station, with Moosie cursing at the police for not helping them.

They wandered all day searching everywhere, and asking everybody they came across, but no luck. "We canny go hame without her," said Jamie, "but maybe she has found her way home to the tent."

So, eagerly they made their way home to the tent, but no, there was no sign of Winkins there.

They sat round the fire all night hoping she would come home, but she never appeared. They searched for days, until one day a policeman came to the tent. "We think we have found your wee girl. She was wandering around and was found by some nuns, and put into a home. I doubt you'll get her back now. Neglect, they said, she wasn't looked after properly."

"That's no' true," said Belle, "she is the apple of our eye. We love her to bits, and want her back."

"You are in no position to demand anything," said the policeman. "If you come with me, there are a few papers for you to sign regarding the little girl."

"What papers?" asked Moosie.

"You will see when you come down to the station."

So they had to follow the policeman down to the police station. When they got there the sergeant was behind his big desk. "Here are the tinks you sent me for, sir."

"You can stand, I don't want to catch anything from you folk. Now, about this little girl you say belongs to you. She is in the orphanage with the Sisters of Mercy, and we want you to sign her over to them, and they will find a good home for her."

"What!" shouted Moosie, "that is our little girl, and we are not giving her up, never in a thousand years."

"You have no choice, my man, I am afraid, but to make your cross here," said the sergeant, pointing to the paper.

"I would rather cut my hand off than make my cross anywhere you tell me. So you can bugger off, and give us back our wee lassie!"

"Did you swear at me, you tink?"

"Aye, and I will do more than that, you low-life bastard!"

No sooner had he said that than Moosie was arrested and got two years hard labour. Belle had to go and stay with her mother and father. She never got Winkins back, and mourned for her for the rest of her life.

Now that was the kind of things that happened to travellers long ago. They had no rights at all, and just got stepped on. It was an aunt of my father's this happened to. It is a true story.

The Dog

This is a very short story I got from an old traveller woman up north, in about 1965.

An old woman and her man were camped up north near Ullapool. Tam was the man's name, and his wife was Kate.

The travellers who were camped next to them had a dog which had a litter of pups – just mongrels. The folk were moving the next day, and were going to drown the pups, because there were nine of them, too many to look after.

When the man came back after doing this cruel deed, his wife said to him, "You have missed one, it crawled away and was hiding among the grass."

When Tam, the old man from the other camp, heard this, he said, "What did you do wi' the puppies?"

"I drooned them, there was too many to look efter. I suppose I'll go down and get rid of this one, tae."

"No, no," said Tam, "we will take it off your hands."

"Fine," said the man. "Are you ready to go, auld wife?"

"Yes, as soon as I give them the pup." She put the wee puppy into Kate's hands, and said goodbye.

"This wee creature will starve to death. How are we going to feed it without its mother?" said Tam.

"We will think of something," said Kate. They looked about until they found a bird's feather, dipped it in some milk and the pup sucked on it. They kept giving the pup the milk till the milk was all gone, and it fell asleep.

"What are we going to call it?" asked Tam.

"Well," said Kate, "we will call it Feather."

Tam laughed at that. "It's as good a name as any."

It was a quiet wee pup, and wanted cuddles all the time. Three months later it had learned to follow the pram when they were moving, but there was something far wrong with this pup. It was a cross-eyed, buck-toothed puppy, the queerest-looking dog you would ever see. It had brown and white spots, with a narrow chalkers.[1] Its narrow face made its teeth stick out all the further. "Aye," the woman told me, "it wasn't a bonny sight, but we saved its life and we loved it, rank[2] or no."

Two years later, the puppy had grown up, and adored Tam and Kate. It slept on their bed in the tent.

One night Tam went to the pub down the road for a drink. The publican knew him because Tam did work for him from time to time, and so he allowed him into his pub. He stayed longer than he intended, and got home about midnight. All was quiet at the tent, and Kate was asleep, but the dog licked his face when he crawled into the tent.

Tam lit up a cigarette, saying, "I'll have a draw of this fag before I go to sleep, alright, Feather!" However he fell asleep with the fag in his hand, and it started a fire.

Feather went to Kate, barking like mad and licking her face. She woke up and went outside, coughing and spluttering, but Tam heard nothing – he was in the doldrums with drink. The dog finally got him awake and he made it out just in time. But it was too late for Feather. He was burned to death saving Kate and Tam. Poor wee Feather.

They never had another dog for at least ten years.

1. face   2. ugly

The Drunken Piper

This is about a piper away down south in the borders of Scotland.

His name was Sandy, and he was a good piper, but he got a bad name, because he couldn't play the pipes unless he was three sheets to the wind. This made his wife very angry, because he got lippy and abusive with a drink on him, and this prevented him from making any money when he played the streets of the towns or the lay-bys. He used to play to the tourists, and what he made, he spent it on drink. He depended on Nancy to keep things going, and she was fed up with him.

One night she said to him, "That's it, Sandy, we are finished. I am going back to my mother and father, and taking wee Agnes with me." Agnes was their daughter of three years old, and she had Down's syndrome. She was a cute, cheery wee lass.

"You cannae go and leave me, Nancy. We have been thegither for six years."

"Aye, six years of torture, wi' you drinking. I am leaving in the morning."

Sandy was sitting at the fire, and it was a good summer's night, drinking a bottle of beer as usual. As Nancy looked at him, he started choking and spluttering, and threw the bottle down. He was pointing to his mouth and throat, and croaked out, "A wasp!"

He had swallowed a wasp that had got into the bottle somehow. He took off like a whippet, and was running round, and round in circles, gasping for air.

"That will learn you," said Nancy. "I said the drink would kill you. Do you believe me now, hingin stanes?[1]"

He made a breenge[2] at her, but missed her and fell on the grass.

1. testicles   2. rush

169

"Let me see your throat then, baldy heed."

He opened his mouth, and she looked down into it. "O my God almighty, your breath smells like a gruffy[1] sty, where the pigs have been farting all day. You are red rotten, man. Wait till I hold my nose, then I will look."

She covered her nose with a cloth, then looked down his throat. His tongue was twice its usual size, she told him.

"Aye," she said, "you haven't got long to go now, Sandy, my lad, the auld de'il will be here soon to cart you away." She was smiling to herself, because there was nothing wrong with his tongue. She was just saying it to make him panic, to get her own back on him, drunkard that he was.

He looked at her, pointed to his backside, and made a sad face.

"You are wantin a geer,[2] aren't you?" she said, and he nodded his head. "Well, awa' into the bushes and get one, you thickent[3] fool."

He ran into the bushes and was away for ten minutes. Then she heard him scream. She ran to see what was wrong with him. And he was standing with his trousers round his ankles. "The wasp stung me on the arse as it was coming out. It wasn't in my throat at all, you silly woman, but my arse!"

"Let me see, then," she said. "Fool, fool, I kent you weren't wise! You have sat on a bunch of nettles. It wasn't a wasp at all. I am still leaving in the morning."

"Ah, Nancy, you cannae leave me now, after all this that has happened. What would I do without you and wee Agnes?"

"Well, I'll stay," was the reply, "but only if you stop drinking."

So he stopped drinking, and had to teach himself how to play the pipes when he was sober. It took him a few weeks, but he managed it.

1. pig   2. shit   3. stupid

Willie Duff

An old traveller lived in a tent with her son, whose name was Kenny. Her man had died two years before when he fell down a quarry drunk. Although Kenny was a wee bit backward, she idolised him, and he did a lot of work for her round the camp.

They were very, very poor, and the only thing they owned was a billy goat. This animal was useless. It never gave them any milk, but they loved it just the same. They called it after the farmer whose land they stayed on, Willie Duff. He had a beard like the goat, and the goat had a beard like him.

"Now Kenny, I have to go intae the toon for some messages, especially bread, we haven't a slice in the camp," said the woman. "I may be a bit later than usual getting hame, but the farmer Willie Duff is coming to tell us about some work he wants us to do on the farm, so have a nice big fire for him when he comes, because it's a bit nippy the day."

Kenny had a great fire going when the farmer arrived. "Is your mother in, Kenny?"

"Na, na, she's awa' out, but she said she wouldn't be long. She telt me to have a big fire to keep you warm, and that you have to sit and wait for her, she doesn't want to miss you."

Seeing as it was a cold, cold day, the farmer took up the invitation to sit at the big fire Kenny had made. The farmer was so comfortable and cosy and warm, he soon fell asleep by the fire.

Kenny sat opposite watching him. Just then, a flea jumped onto the farmer's brow, and started crawling round his shiny baldy head. Kenny couldn't keep his eyes off the tiny creature.

Finally he couldn't stand it any longer. "Shoo!" said Kenny, "get off the farmer's head!"

171

But the flea took no notice of him, and kept wandering around on the farmer's head.

Kenny tried blowing gently on the farmer's head to see if he could shift it, but it just kept coming back to the same place.

"You are not going to come off, are you, you swine!" Kenny was so obsessed by this flea, he got angry. He grabbed a big stick near the fire, and he cracked it with full force onto the farmer's head, killing him.

At this point, Kenny's mother came home and saw the farmer dead, his head split in two. She knew her son had gone too far this time. Although Kenny was not responsible for his actions, she knew he wouldn't get away with killing someone. The least they would do was to take him away from her and lock him up in some asylum or prison.

She could not bear the thought that she would be parted from her son, and she was determined to save and protect him.

The old woman raked through the farmer's pockets, and found a bag of money. He was carrying it because he had been at the market that day, but had bought nothing.

She put the bag in her pocket, and said to Kenny, "Don't say a word about this if the ploops[1] come." She put the farmer in her tent to hide him from the police, planning to bury him later.

A thought came to her, and she said to Kenny, "You go and get some wood, and I will bury Willie Duff, and no one will ever know."

Her idea was to make Kenny look sillier than he really was, because she knew that if Kenny was asked about the farmer, he would blurt out the truth. When she got the boy away, she dug a hole near the tent, killed the goat and put it in the hole.

"Well," said Kenny when he came back, "did you bury Willie Duff?"

"Aye, lad, I did. Come and see where he is buried," and she showed him the grave.

Two hours later, the police arrived. They said the farmer's wife was worried about her man. She knew he was coming

1. police

172

down to see the tinker woman and her son, and had never come back.

"Have you seen him?" asked the police. "Have you seen Willie Duff?"

Kenny spoke up. "Yes, I killed him. I beat his brains in. Come, I will show you his grave if you don't believe me." Kenny took them down to the grave his mother had dug, and they scraped the sand away with shovels, and came across the dead billy goat.

"Who is that?" they asked Kenny.

"That's Willie Duff," said Kenny.

"There is something funny here," said the police. "Is this the Willie Duff you killed?"

"No, it was Willie Duff the farmer I killed."

The police realised that a trick was being played on them. They arrested the woman and Kenny and took them to jail. After the trial they were both hanged for what they had done.

Too Many Cooks

Here is a short story I got from an old man in Dundee.

Many years ago this man was camped near Arbroath. His cousin and his sister were there, and there were a few other tents. He was glad of the company, as his wife had died two years previously, and he had no bairns.

It was a calm summer's day at the end of August, but there was a nip in the air. The old woman in the next tent to him had a big pot of soup on. He watched her prepare it. Now this woman had a big family, there must have been ten of them at least, so you can imagine the size of the pot.

She went to get more wood for the fire, and her daughter arrived. She took a spoon and stirred the pot, Then she went over to where the salt was and added a handful to the soup. She looked at the old man and said "My mother never puts salt in the soup. So I've done it." Fair enough, thought the old man.

About ten minutes later a young man came into the camp, lifted the spoon, stirred the soup, and put a handful of salt in it. The old man was smirking to himself, but said nothing.

Then the old woman came back, and put sticks on the fire. She looked at the old man. "Well," said she, "my family are always complaining about me not putting salt in anything, so I had better add some," and she took a big handful of salt and put it in the pot, then stirred it up, and put the lid back on. The reason none of them tasted the soup off the spoon to see how salty it was, was that no travellers would do that, because we would say we were slavering in the soup, and we don't do it.

The old man went and got a sandwich and made a cup of tea. Then he sat by his fire, waiting for the fun to start. They all came home near to five o'clock, and sat down waiting for their soup. The old woman took out a bing[1] of cups and ladled the soup into them, and handed them all a cup of soup. They waited a while, because it was too hot to drink straight away. Then she handed round the bread to steep in the soup. When they thought it was cool enough, they took a big swig of it, one after the other.

Well, the old man never saw folk move so fast in his life. They were spluttering and coughing all over the place, and some were vomiting. The old man had to go into his tent with laughing. They were all ill for a few days – too ill to enquire who had spoiled the soup.

The old man looked at me and said, "You see, lass, it's true – too many cooks does spoil the broth!" He was still laughing as I walked away. He shouted after me, "And that's the end of my story!"

1. lot

Courage

Meckie was a young girl in her early twenties. Her name was really Mary, but she got Meckie instead. She had had a very hard life of it with her mother and father, who were always fighting and drinking. She had one brother aged fourteen, and her sister was twelve. Meckie had had to bring them up. Her parents ignored their children, because they had Meckie to look after them. They never worried about it.

Meckie swore she would never, ever, get married. She thought to herself, if that's all married people do is to argue all the time, no, it wasn't for her.

She liked nothing better than to run barefooted among the grass, with the long grass going between her toes. The feeling of freedom of that was unbelievable. If only folk would try it, she thought to herself. It is a contentment that floods over you. It was her granny who had told her about it. She said it would relieve stress and worry, and it worked for Meckie.

Meckie was born in 1900, and was bullied by her father. Her mother wasn't bad to her, but she was frightened of the father, so what he said went. Meckie's granny, her mother told her, was an old spaewife. She read the hands, and could tell the future, and she had cures for illnesses. She told fortunes by looking into the eyes, her mother told her. Meckie's father objected to her mother speaking about the granny. He called her an old witch, perhaps because the granny thought he wasn't good enough for her daughter. None of the kids ever saw their granny, because she died when Meckie was young.

Down at the bottom of the field where they stayed there were some sheep and lambs. Meckie wandered down there every second day and stroked and played with them, and fed them bread. When they saw her coming, they all came to the fence to meet her. She had a way with animals and children.

One morning she arrived at the fence where the lambs and sheep were, and there was a lot of blood all over it. Meckie panicked and ran up to the farmer to tell him. The farmer came down to have a look, and he found that one of the wee lambs was missing.

"Maybe it was a dog got it," said Meckie.

"No, it was nae dog," said the farmer. "There is no bits of carcass, only plenty of blood. It was done by a human, I am afraid. Where was your father last night, Mary?"

"As usual he was at the pub, and we were sleeping by the time he came hame. He never done it, Mr Farmer. He wouldn't."

"Well, Mary, he has done it before, about five years ago, but this time he won't get aff sae light. I have to get the police in on it. Sorry, Mary."

Mary ran home to tell her father that the feekies[1] were coming. "What for?" asked the father.

"For choring[2] a wee lamb," said Meckie.

Her father dived into the tent and came out with a parcel that was all stained with blood, and ran across the field with it in his arms, cursing and swearing all the way.

Her mother said, "He had to do it, Meckie, to feed you bairns."

"If he didn't drink so much, he would have the money to feed us," said Meckie. Her mother slapped her on the face. "Dinnae speak about your faither like that, lassie. You are an ungrateful bitch, that you are."

Meckie could see that her mother was half cut with drink herself, and wasn't thinking straight. "Oh, the cursed drink," thought Meckie. "Maybe they will get the jail for this, this time. Serves them right if they do."

They waited round the fire for the feekies to arrive, and in about half an hour they came. "Well, well, what is this you have

1. police   2. stealing

been up to, Willie? Stealing sheep again? Do you know I can have you hanged for this?"

Willie's face went pure white. "I did nothing," said Willie.

"Oh come on, now, we know you did."

Meckie stepped forward. "I did it, to feed my wee sister and brother," and she hung her head down. "I was always down at the sheep – ask the farmer, he caught me often playing wi' them."

"Well," said the constable, "if you say you did it, then so be it, a confession is acceptable, even if you didn't do it." The mother and father did nothing, but kept silent. "Come on then, lass, let's go."

Meckie was taken to the police station, and had to sit for two hours till the Inspector came in from his break. "Now what have we got here?" he said, looking at Meckie.

"My name is Mary Stuart, sir."

"Well, Mary Stuart, and what were you up to?"

"I stole a lamb to feed the family, sir. We were hungry."

"You know what you can get for doing that, Mary Stuart?"

"Yes, sir, I was told."

"Are you no' frightened, Mary?"

"No, sir, I am not. What God puts in front of you, you have to accept it, and do your punishment."

The inspector smiled to himself, and turned his back on her. Turning round slowly again, he stared at her. "Lock her up, constable."

Meckie was taken and put in a cell that stank to high heaven of beer, and there was sloosh[1] in the corner. She sat down on a stool that was there, and waited to see what was going to happen to her. She started thinking up all sort of things. Maybe she would hang, maybe she would be taken in a boat to a far-off country, or she might be raped by the police. No, no, her imagination was running away with her. Nothing could be worse than that.

---

1. urine

She lay in the cell all night, and got bread and water for her supper. She didn't touch it. In the morning, about seven o clock, she heard the clink of keys and the constable came in. "This way, Mary Stuart."

She followed him to the front office, where the inspector was sitting at his desk. "It will be two months till a judge gets here from Edinburgh to try you. I can't keep you in the cells that long, so I am putting you in the orphanage to work with the children till then, but you must behave yourself."

"Thank God," Meckie thought. "Nae hanging, nae going on a big boat, *and nae rape*. Phew. It's no' bad after all."

She was taken to the orphanage, and settled in there fine and made friends with the staff and children. There was a man there who helped her a lot to begin with. He was about forty, and his name was Duncan Monroe.

When the judge came, he gave her the penalty that she must return to the orphanage, and she had to stay there. The Inspector came to tell her the news, and she thanked him. God knows where her mother and family were now, she thought. They had cleared out when she was lifted.

"Aye," said the Inspector, "You have courage, Mary Stewart."

"Yes," she said. She was soon to become Mrs Monroe. Meckie and her man stayed at the orphanage till they both died of old age, and there was a plaque put up in their memory, for working there so long.

Sandy and Meg

The rain was pouring down, and it awoke Meg and Sandy with the noise it made on the canvas tent.

"I hope we don't get flooded," said Sandy, "like last year when we were here."

"Och, stop griping, Sandy. You sound like an auld woman wi' your moaning."

"I am no' an auld woman, and I never will be. God help you if I changed. Who wid tickle your fancy then, eh, Meg?" and he tickled her in the ribs.

"Awa' wi' you, you silly auld git. Go oot and see the condition o' the tent."

So Sandy went out to see what like the tent was from the outside. "It seams to be fine, Meg. Nae disasters the day, and it has stopped raining, thank God."

Meg got up and went and put the kettle on, after Sandy had built the fire.

"Them wee buggers, Sandy, they have rummaged all through my groceries I bought yesterday, and stolen all the breed."

"Who did?" asked Sandy.

"Them thick-lippet dugs o' yours. I will swing for them yet, I will," said Meg.

"What have we got to eat, then, Meg?"

"Nitchels.¹"

"We will just have to wait till we get tae the shops again, and buy breed."

"What with, shirt buttons? We have nae loor.²"

Sandy laughed. "Well, you will just have to go and hawk the hooses for breed."

1. nothing   2. money

180

So off they went to the wee village down the road. As they were passing a wee wood, they heard a scream coming from it.

"What's that? Listen," and they heard it again.

"Somebody is in trouble, Sandy, go see."

"No' me," said Sandy. "It may be a ghost."

"Oh, for God's sake, Sandy, you are moich.[1] Run, lappert concern,[2] I will go and see."

"I will come wi' you," said Sandy.

Meg shook her head and climbed the fence, with Sandy at her heels. They followed the noise of whimpering, and came across a woman, waist-deep in a bog.

"Oh, thank God you heard me," she said. "I am well and truly stuck, and can't pull myself out."

"We will try and help you," Sandy said. "Meg, you run back to the camp and get my rope that's behind the tent."

"Aye, fairly I will – you go yourself and get it."

"But Meg –" She gave him a funny look, and he said no more, and ran off to get the rope himself. He was back in ten minutes with a thick rope. "Here, lassie, tie it roon your waist, and we will have you oot in a minute."

They pulled the woman out of the bog, and she lay on the grass panting. "I have been stuck there for two hours, and my horse fled. It will have gone back home. I can't thank you enough for saving me. Please come with me, and have your breakfast with me at least."

So they went with the woman to her house, and what a house it was – a mansion on an estate. They followed the woman up the drive, and a gentleman came running out. "Oh my dear, the horse came back without you. I was so worried!"

"I am fine, my dear, thanks to these two people, they saved me," said the woman.

He stepped forward and thanked them for what they had done, and ushered them into the kitchen where they ate their fill. A few minutes later the lady came back and said to them,

1. mad   2. stupid person

"Take this as a token of my appreciation for saving me," and she handed them a five pound note, a lot of money in those days.

Just then Sandy gave a shout, and woke up.

"Get up out of there, you lazy auld gadgie[1] and light the fire for wir tea," said Meg.

"But we have nae breed for to eat."

"Wha said that?" asked Meg.

"You did – you said the dogs ate it all."

"What dogs? We have nae dogs, fool."

"But… but…" and then he stopped. He had been dreaming again, as usual.

"You are a thickent[2] auld man, you live in a dream world. Here, have your tea. I have made toast for you, lazy gouls.[3]"

He lay back in the bed, mulling over his dream. He wished he had that fiver the lady had given him.

"Silly me," he said to himself. "Ah well," he thought, "we can live on wir dreams, it's all we have."

"Get up, dreamer boy, and we will go hawking, and try and get some money before we leave here."

They packed up their tent, and put it on the pram with the tent sticks. That evening they left, and Sandy took his dreams with him.

1. fellow   2. daft   3. arse

Tam Soutar

There was a man called Tam Soutar, and he was a man who mortally hated travellers. He had a wee shop in a small village in Angus. This was in 1893. There were tinkers used to camp near the wee village, and they stayed there in the winter months. The shop didn't make much money, and Tam couldn't turn away the tinkers' custom, so he just put up with them, but he hated it. If a tinker came into his shop, rather than go and serve them, he sent his wife. When she wasn't there, he was forced to serve them, most reluctantly.

One day his wife was at the market, buying stock for the shop, and he was in the shop himself. A young tinker boy came into the shop for some bread and tobacco for his granny.

"Does your granny still smoke that disgusting clay pipe of hers? A very bad habit, especially for a woman."

"Yes, she does, and what business is it of yours what my old granny does, Mr Soutar?"

"Don't you be so cheeky, my boy, or I will have the police on to you."

"What for, Mr Soutar – or Mr Sourpuss, as the whole village calls you? You are not very liked in these parts, are you? That is why some people go to the next village for messages, and I can't blame them either."

That night, when Tam Soutar went to his bed, he thought over what the tinker boy had said. He thought to himself, "Maybe that boy is right – maybe I am taking this tinker thing too far. I am a God-fearing man, and I go to the church every Sunday regular as clockwork, but I sleep through the whole service, and I never hear a word the minister says. Next Sunday I am going to listen to what he says, be it good or bad."

The next day he woke up feeling all sick and dizzy, and his wife was left in charge of the shop that day. The tinkers liked it when she was in the shop on her own. She was a nice woman, was Mrs Soutar, and if she had any stottin bits (food they didn't want any more) she used to give it to Rachel, a young traveller girl that came in. Rachel was a bonny girl, but she had very bad skin, all rough and like sandpaper. She was a nice lass, but very, very shy. When Tam was in the shop, he made her stand at the door and shout in what she wanted, because he said he didn't want to catch a disease off her.

Two days after this, Rachel died. A horse and cart had overturned and fallen on her. Her parents were distraught, and it was just before Christmas.

Mrs Soutar just couldn't stop crying about the death of poor Rachel. That didn't please her man. "Why are you wasting your tears over that scabby tinker lassie?"

In a moment Mrs Soutar stopped crying, braced herself, lifted a knife, and stuck it in Mr Soutar's arm. He fell back in agony, blood streaming down his clothes. Then he tumbled to the floor.

Stiff-faced, she put on her shawl, walked out of the shop and went to the police station. She walked in and said, "I have stabbed my husband."

She sat down on a chair, and it just came to her what she had done. Then she smiled and turned to the constable. "What a relief, I should have done it years ago."

The policeman looked at her, then turned to the other constable, pointing to his brow and making a screwing motion, as if to say she had gone mad.

They took Tam to the doctor, and put her in the jail. His wound wasn't deep, and the doctor let him go home. Mrs Soutar was allowed home as well. They said it was a family squabble, so she wasn't charged with anything.

After she got home, he arrived half an hour later with a bandage on his arm. She had his bags all packed and laid on the step at the door.

"What's this?" he said to her.

"It's your things. You are not staying with me another minute, you evil, dirty, dirty man that you are. That poor tinker lass that never did you any harm in your life, you thought it was good she was killed. She was my friend!"

She made a run at him, but he dodged her and went behind a chair.

"I am going to tell everyone why you hate travellers so much – it's because you are one yourself, and you have been hiding it from this village for too long. I am going to tell all," she said.

"I was trying to better myself, because of the feelings of the non-travellers towards us," was his reply.

"Well, you are packed up now, go!"

He looked at her and knew she was not kidding, so he left. He had lost everything – wife, shop and house – and he had not a penny, she kept it all. It was her shop anyway.

He ended up in the small wood where the travellers lived, but at the other end of it, in a bow tent. The village was a better place without Tam Soutar.

Soutar wasn't his name anyway. He had taken the name from his wife. He was Tam Stewart.

Mary the Bully

Fifty years ago there was a girl in a travelling family called Mary, and all she lived for was to bully everyone she met, be it child, adult, cat, dog, anything at all.

Her family were camped near Brechin. It was the berry-picking time, and she and her family were picking every day.

One day Mary went about wakening up all the kids that were asleep in their prams. She did it sneaky-like, and no one saw her, but her mother and father knew it was her.

"What are we going to do about that lassie o' ours?" said her mother to her father.

"I just don't know. Maybe if she got a fright of some kind, that would stop her."

"Yes, we will try that, but you know she isn't easy frightened."

They thought about it for a few days, and couldn't think of anything.

There came a day when Mary was worse than ever. She bullied everyone at the campsite. The father and mother were now desperate.

"Well," said the father, "I know what we will do – we will take her someplace and dump her. That should frighten her."

"Mary hasn't much sense of direction," said her mother, "so that would be easy."

They hitched up the horse and cart and they climbed into it with Mary. They said they were going to the town for groceries. Mary loved going through the shops causing havoc.

They took her to a strange part of the town that they had never been to before, and her mother said to Mary, "Go to that house, Mary, and ask for some boiling water for a drop tea."

Mary got the kettle and went up a close to the house. When she was out of sight, the father jumped off the cart and led the horse round the corner. Then he jumped on again and made off faster than he had ever gone before.

At the door of the house there was a red-striped cat lying on the doorstep. Mary lifted her foot and started teasing the cat by nudging it with her foot till it ran off screeching. Mary was laughing hysterically, when the door opened and a very tall red-haired woman stood there. "What do you want?" said the woman.

"Could you give me some boiling water for some tea for my mother and father?" said Mary. She had never said please in her life, and the woman thought her rather brazen, but didn't say anything. She went in to put the kettle on, and Mary wandered about kicking every stone in her path defiantly. Then she noticed the horse and cart were gone, and her mother and father were nowhere to be seen.

Mary started shouting, "Ma, Da, where the hell are you?" but only silence met her ears. She ran round shouting like a mad woman till she became exhausted, and sat down on a bench with her head in her hands. Her anger was swelling up in her, so she got up again and stamped away down the street till she met an old man.

"Hi, man," she shouted to him, "where are the tinkers' camps around here?"

The old man showed her the way, and grinning to herself she headed in the direction the man pointed out. Eventually she came to the camp. kicking every dog in her path and nipping the children's ears till they screamed.

Her mother and father were sitting around the fire, and looked up when a child screamed. "Oh my God," said the father, "she is back too soon. I don't think she has learned her lesson."

She came charging into the camp and kicked the fire till it scattered all over the place, sparks flying everywhere. "She is worse," said the mother.

Mary's brother Johnny crept up to his mother and said, "Ma, I ken what she is feart of – there's only one thing, water."

The father looked up with startled eyes. "That's it," he said, and he dashed off and went round the tents, preparing a plot to cure Mary once and for all of her bullying. Everyone was to come to his tent at eight that night.

They all arrived at exactly that time to carry out their plot. The men grabbed Mary, and with the women following behind they all went down to the river and threw Mary in. She couldn't swim and was screaming her head off, but her father told her she had to promise never to bully again. If she promised, he would save her, or they would do the same thing every night till she learned her lesson. Choking and spluttering, she agreed. She was fished out of the river that night, and never bullied ever again.

Papplers

Tam Stirling was a grumpy man, he never had a good word to say about anybody – and greedy, oh my God, he wouldn't give you a drink of water out of his can, suppose you were dying of thirst.

His wife was Agnes, and he had one laddie, Hughie. How he ever got a wife puzzled all the travellers at that time. She was a gentle wee woman, not very pretty, but she had a smile that would melt your heart. Hughie was a laddie who never did what his father told him, he thought his father was a fool.

One day his father was going out hawking, but there was no porridge. They had no oatmeal in the camp, and this put him in a foul mood. "Hi, laddie, go to the shop and get some meal for my papplers.[1]"

"Awa', you silly auld man and go yourself. I'm no' your skivvy."

Agnes said she would go to the shop, and off she went. Hours passed, and she didn't come back. Hughie was worried about his old mother, but his father said, "It would be like her to bide away, and never come back."

"How can you say that, Dad? She is a good woman."

She never came back that night, and in the morning Hughie said he was going to look for her. He went to the village, and folk said they saw her going into the shop, but never saw her come out. This worried him, and he went to the police station and reported her missing.

"Your mother, missing?" said the policeman, and he laughed. "Who would kidnap that auld hen? Unless to eat her," and the other policeman laughed with him.

1. porridge

189

Disgusted, Hughie walked out of the police station, and thought, "I will find her myself."

He wandered all day, and went to various places that other travellers were staying, but he couldn't find his mother. He headed home, because it was getting very dark.

His father was sitting at the fire with a horrible look of anger on his face. "I had to go to the shop myself to get the meal. She never came back, the stupid woman that she is!"

"Father, maybe there is something wrong. What could have happened to my mother?"

"I don't give a damn for her. Your tole[1] is in the pan, you will have to heat it up again."

"Bugger you and your tole, I want none of it."

Next morning Hughie said he was going out again to search for his mother. He wandered to the village, and a man came over to him and said, "I saw your mother this morning, Hughie."

"Where, where?"

"Two miles from here, in a camp with another man."

"What!"

"Yes, and I will tell you where she is for a half crown."

Hughie gave the man half a crown and went where he told him to go. When he got there, there was no tent, no mother and no man. He had given away the half crown for nothing.

He went home, and there, sitting round the fire, were his mother and father.

"Where have you been, mother? I have been searching for you for two days."

"Don't be silly, boy, I have been here all the time."

"Mother, you went for meal, and didn't come back."

"I will have to put him to bed, Tam, he is moich.[2]"

So off he went to bed to rest, and he slept for a whole day. When he woke up, his mother asked him how he was feeling.

"I am fine, Mam, but where were you the last two days?"

She shook her head and said nothing.

For two days he went on and on about her being away.

1. skirlie   2. mad

They decided to move from that camp for a wee while, thinking it might help Hughie to forget the whole thing. They decided to go and camp ten miles away where Tam's sister was camped. She was a great woman for telling fortunes and the like. They thought maybe she could have a word with Hughie, to see what was wrong with him.

That night, she had a long talk with him, but came to no conclusion.

Through the night he took ill as if he was in a fit or something. He was in his own tent, so there was no one to help him, and in the morning he had died. They sent for the police, and they came with a doctor, and he was pronounced dead.

Why he died the doctor didn't know. There was nobody in those days to say what he died of, and it wasn't pursued.

I got this story from a member of the family. It was handed down to her. Many of the family said the father poisoned him, but what really happened has never been known to this day.

Deaf Maggie

*This is a story I got from Deaf Maggie's grand-niece. It happened in
1897, and was a great tragedy to the family at the time, and was never
forgotten.*

There was a wee girl born into a family of travellers who was a
perfect baby. They called her Margaret, but Maggie for short.
She was the first girl in the family for many years. Up to then
there were all boys, and you can imagine the joy it gave the
family having a wee girl.

When Maggie was aged twelve she was struck down with a
virus. She was ill for a long time, and when she recovered she
was left deaf. She had taken a mastoid ear, and would never be
able to hear again. This was a great tragedy, but she could still
speak.

This was sad enough, but worse was to come. When she was
sixteen she was raped by a young man, and fell pregnant. She
didn't tell her mother, because she didn't know what was the
matter with her.

Her baby was born a boy, and he was deformed. His legs were
twisted, and his head shook all the time, but he was a lovely wee
boy. She called him Sandy, after her father. The family pulled
together and helped her bring up the child. When Sandy was
learning to talk they found out he had an impediment in his
speech. His tongue was too long for his mouth, poor thing that
he was. But he was loved and happy.

They moved from where they were camping and went
further south, to somewhere where they thought the weather
was better. They went to a town that had a horse fair. This was
the old father's pride and joy, he loved horses.

They arrived and pitched their tents, and settled down for the night. They were getting funny looks from some of the other travellers when they saw Sandy – he had to be carried at all times.

At two in the morning there was a fight broke out not far from their tent, and men and women were roaring like bulls. Maggie couldn't hear the noise, but Sandy did and was crying and touching his mother's face. His granny and granddad heard it. The fight was about a horse that wasn't paid for. One man said he had paid for it, and had it on a rope, and the other man said it wasn't paid for.

So they had started to fight, and the horse got a fright and bolted. This was right in front of Maggie's tent; the horse crashed into the tent and trampled it to the ground. Everyone got up to see what was happening. Sandy was screaming, then the screaming stopped suddenly.

Sandy's granny and grandad lifted the tent that had been flattened, with Sandy and Maggie under it. In a panic they ripped it off. There lay poor Sandy and Maggie. She was conscious but he was not, and his nose was bleeding.

They pulled him out from under the tent, and Maggie got out by herself, but was very shaky. A young boy said he would run for the doctor who stayed nearby. When the doctor came and looked at Sandy, he said, "I must take this boy to the hospital, he is in a bad way."

The doctor took Sandy in his horse and cart, and took him to the hospital, which was where he had his surgery. He was still unconscious. There was a print of the horse's hoof on the side of his head. The family waited in a waiting room. Then the doctor came out, and said he was sorry, but Sandy had passed away.

It was as if all hell had broken loose. The family were devastated. The granny turned to her man and said, "Someone has put a curse on us, old man. That's the only explanation I have for all our troubles. We are the unluckiest, insantifit[1] family that

1. cursed

ever lived on this earth. Now poor Sandy is dead, and he never had a life at all." Then she burst out crying, as did the rest of them.

They buried Sandy at the end of a field, because travellers weren't allowed in a graveyard, and they had no money for the burial. The grandfather dug his grave and they laid Sandy to rest.

They headed back up north again, a very sad family. A few months later Maggie's father was arrested for being drunk and disorderly, which was a very, very, bad crime for a traveller in these days. They took him out and hanged him in public, and put Maggie and her mother in the stocks, so that they were publicly humiliated. They were kept in the stocks for two days, then were let loose and stoned out of the town.

Maggie's mum died a week later, and Maggie threw herself in the river and drowned herself. That was a whole family wiped out through no fault of their own, only because they were travellers. In those days, according to the non-traveller, travellers had no right to live.

That story never died, and was kept alive by Sandy's brothers and sisters. The family mourn them to this day. It was a horrible tragedy for one family.

The Lord's Prayer

This next story shows how important travellers' knowledge is to them. They work out things using their brains and through their skills, and really can rely on their wits. This story is based on that. It has a great moral to it, and it is true.

There was a traveller man, and he was walking away up in the north of Scotland. Now, if you have been up there, you will understand what a lonely and God-forsaken part of the country it is. He was starving with hunger, he hadn't eaten for a few days, the soles of his shoes were worn right down to the road, and the blisters on his feet were the size of eggs. He was in a terrible state.

He was walking up a part of the glen with a long stretch of road in front of him. He stopped and looked up, and coming towards him was another traveller man. He thought to himself, "Thank God, here is another man coming. I thought I was the only person left on the planet."

He was so glad to see somebody else he shook hands with him, and bade him good day. "Thank God I have met you. You wouldn't have any thing to eat in your pocket, would you, or a cigarette? I haven't eaten for a few days, and my belly is sore with the hunger."

"No, I am sorry, but I am hungry myself. I haven't eaten either."

"Well, is there any houses up here I could beg for a sandwich or something to eat?"

"Yes, there is a manse about half a mile up the road, but for God's sake don't go there. He is a beast of a man, and he will set the dog on you."

195

"I will have to try it – must is a hard master. Thank you," he said, and he walked on up the hill.

Sure enough, a half mile up the road there stood the house. There were two big gates, and a sign saying 'Manse'.

In he went through the big gates, and knocked on the door. A butler answered his knock, and said to him, "What can I do for you, my man?"

"Well, sir, I have come to see the minister, and I am not here to beg. I was told he is the best minister in Scotland, and I have come here for him to teach me something."

So in the butler went and brought out the minister.

"Well," said the minister, "I hear you want to see me."

"Oh yes, your reverence. I have heard you are the best minister in Scotland, and I have travelled for days to come and see you, so that you can teach me something."

The minister threw out his chest a bit at the compliment. "Well, what do you want me to teach you, my man?"

"Well, your reverence, I want you to teach me the Lord's Prayer," said the traveller.

"Don't you know the Lord's Prayer, my man?"

"No, sir, I never learned it."

"Very well," said the minister, "I will teach you," and he began: "Our Father…"

"Hold on a minute," said the traveller man. "Did you say Our Father?"

"Yes, I did," said the minister.

"So that means to say he is your father?"

"Yes, he is."

"Well, if he is your father, he must be my father."

"Of course he is."

"Well, if he is your father and he is my father, we must be two brothers."

"Yes, putting it that way, we are."

"Well, would you see your brother go with an empty belly, and me not ate for days?"

The minister gave a wee smile. "Very well, I will take you round the back, and ask cook to feed you."

The cook put out a big plate of meat for him, and he got tucked into it, and what was left he put it in his handkerchief for later.

"Well," said the traveller man, "You are a great cook. Thank you, but I must see the minister again."

Off the cook goes, and comes back with the minister.

"Have you had a good feed, my man?" asked the minister.

"A wonderful feed, your reverence, thank you, but you still haven't taught me the Lord's Prayer."

"No, I haven't had a chance, so we will start again then, shall we?"

The traveller man nodded, and the minister began: "Our Father..."

The traveller man put up his hand to stop the minister from saying any more, and said, "Excuse me, your reverence, but is he still your father?"

"But of course."

"And he is still my father?"

"Yes."

"Well, if he is still your father, and my father, are we still brothers?"

"Of course we are."

"Well, would you see your brother going with a pair of boots like this, with no soles in them, and blisters the size of eggs, and the blood running out of them?"

Again the minister gave a wee smile. "Alright, but looking at your feet my shoes wouldn't fit you. So take this note down to the cobbler in the village, and get a pair of boots, and tell him I will be down in a few days to pay for them."

So off the traveller man goes, as happy as a lark. He went down to the cobblers and chose the best leather boots he had in the shop, and away he went.

Now, a few days later, when the minister was having his

afternoon tea, a thought came to him: "I must go down and pay for that traveller man's boots. I forgot all about it." He put on his coat and went down to the village, and into the cobbler's.

The cobbler looked up when the small bell rang that was above the door. When he saw it was the minister, he stopped what he was doing and said, "Good afternoon, your reverence. I haven't seen you in a long time."

"No, and I haven't seen you in a long time either, John."

"Ah well, I have been so busy with work. What with making boots and shoes for the village and the big house, and of course that traveller man's boots, I haven't had time to come to church."

"Ah, but you must always make time to come to church, you know, John."

The cobbler hung his head.

"Now," said the minister, "with you not coming to the church lately, do you still remember the Lord's Prayer?"

"Of course I do."

"Well, would you mind quoting it to me?"

"Of course, your reverence, everyone knows the Lord's Prayer," and he started, "Our Father…"

"Hold on a minute," said the minister. "Did you say 'our father'?"

"Yes," said the cobbler.

"So that means he is your father?"

"Yes, of course."

"Well, if he is your father, he must be my father."

"Yes."

"Well, if he is your father, and he is my father, he must be that traveller man's father as well?"

"Well, putting it that way, your reverence, yes he is."

"So, if he is your father and my father, and that travelling man's father, we must be three brothers."

"Yes, I suppose we are."

"Well, you pay for one half of your brother's boots, and I'll pay for the other."